OFFICE
Date

#1 *New York Times* Bestselling Author
RACHEL VAN DYKEN

Office Date
by Rachel Van Dyken

Copyright © 2022 RACHEL VAN DYKEN

OFFICE DATE
Copyright © 2022 RACHEL VAN DYKEN
ISBN: 978-1-957700-06-9
Cover Design by Letitia Hasser, r.b.a. Designs
Editing by Kay Springsteen
Formatting & Editing by Jill Sava, Love Affair With Fiction

DEDICATION

To Thor,

Thanks for sitting up with me in your fort so we could finish
this book together.
PS love your flashlight. ☺

CHAPTER
One

Ivy

The flyer clearly said applicants wanted for a brand-new marketing firm under Emory Enterprises.

That's it, the end.

Or maybe that's just the beginning.

I wasn't homeless yet, but it was looking to go that way post-graduation—why did nobody ever warn me about life after college? I mean, I vaguely remember my grandma giving me a lecture on how important it was to pick a major that would guarantee me a job post-graduation—but I also remember her smoking a ton of weed while she was going through chemo *soooooooo* some things got lost in translation.

Apparently, a lot of things.

Like when I found the chihuahua in the toilet because she wanted to give it a bath and the bathtub was too large, and she was afraid it would give him nightmares. Or the multiple times I found her sitting on the couch eating chips and going on and on about Baywatch and how she could one hundred percent fit in a red bikini better than The Rock or Zac Efron.

So, it's not like I truly paid attention when she said at one point that all of this was important, well, until the pink flier and the fact that I double majored in piano performance and music.

I wince at the sound of stapling a piece of blank paper fills the air, and then I sigh. After applying for the internship, I was shocked when I actually got the job along with ten other interns.

And it was a paid internship!

I'd already mentally spent all the money I was going to earn by my first day, but by day twelve, I was ready to commit murder.

And it was all his fault.

Staple.

Staple.

Staple.

Newsflash, basically everything we do is digital, but he clearly remembered that things like stapling and nails going down a chalkboard trigger me past the point of sanity.

Staple.

Staple.

Must he hit it so hard?

What the hell is he even stapling?

All of our desks are in the same area of the office, the newbie area, and lucky us, the CEO doesn't believe in cubicles, so everyone can see everyone and hear everything.

I can still smell the tuna from Anderson four desks down.

My row of five desks faces the other row of five with a nice little community area in the middle with coffee, snacks, and a nice little conference table.

And yet I still hear the staples being punched into the paper.

I didn't know when I took this internship that he would too. My old next-door neighbor, childhood nemesis, high school bully, and college crush.

It was a slight crush, but he'd really filled out, and I hadn't recognized him, so I hit on him… he kissed me then said he didn't date girls like me.

Whatever the hell that meant.

He then grabbed another girl's hand and took her upstairs. After that, the party was a blur except for puking up those little Jack in the Box tacos into the toilet and watching them swirl down toward the ocean to meet Nemo.

It's his fault I can't even eat Jack in the Box anymore!

Not that it matters since his name is, in fact, Jack; should have been a huge beaming neon sign in front of that one. My roommate at the time said that I was so sad about his rejection I wanted to actually eat him.

Thus, the tacos.

Staple.

Staple.

Staple.

I finally look up.

Jack's green eyes lock onto mine as he continues to staple what looks like blank paper

Over. And Over. And Over. AND OVER.

"Shouldn't you be working?" I snap.

He staples again, his annoyingly sexy smirk looking hotter and hotter, damn him. "This is work."

"You're costing the company a shit ton of money in unnecessary staples." I smile, my lips tremble at the sides because it's so hard to actually keep it frozen like that when I want to rage. "Don't you think?"

He staples again. "No, I think I'm good."

He has no business having such pretty green eyes that almost look like he's wearing eyeliner, they're so intense. He has gorgeous long black eyelashes and perfectly manicured fingernails, which is a weird thing to fixate on, but because of the staples, I can't look away.

Bet he could do a lot with just one of those fingers.

Stop it!

I take a deep breath. "What are you working on that needs so many aggressive staples?"

Swear if he staples one more time...

Staple.

I jump to my feet; the scrape of my chair being shoved backward fills the room as the rest of the interns look over at us in interest; then again, this is a regular occurrence or has been since we all started working.

"Jack." I grit my teeth. "Why do you have to be so hateful?"

"Why do you have to be so loud?" he counters quickly. "I'm doing my job, and all you're doing is standing there... wearing..." He frowns. "But seriously, what are you wearing?"

I self-consciously look down at my older pair of black heels, my black tights, and matching black dress with my white tuxedo jacket.

I literally clutch the pearls around my neck—the ones my grandma gave me—and want to hurl them at him, but then I wouldn't have them anymore, and I never take them off.

I haven't since her death.

Never will, I think.

"And now she's clutching her pearls, literally." He sighs.

"You look like you went into your grandma's closet, raided it, and came out with the worst possible outfit."

It stung because it was true.

She'd helped raise me.

And I didn't exactly have work-appropriate clothes, so I raided pieces from her closet that were too precious to toss out or donate.

I bite back tears of anger and hurt.

"Jack," Anderson says from his spot down the line. "Lay off it for today, yeah? It's almost time for happy hour anyway."

"Like she ever comes," Jack mumbles and starts to staple again.

I swipe my cheek and slowly slump back into my chair and stare at my laptop screen as it continues to blur in front of me.

"Boss is here!" One of the receptionists rushes around the corner in her heels, nearly colliding with my desk. "Get your badges on now!"

We all fumble for the badges we keep in our desks and put them on as fast as possible, even staple boy.

I quickly check my face in selfie mode and set my phone down only to catch Jack doing the same. As if he has anything out of place; the guy's a walking magazine spread, and I mean that literally.

He's also so rich I'm actually offended he's working with me. Can't he just work for his dad or something? Become a lawyer for his firm?

I've spent way too much time thinking about it, and stress is bad for my soul, so I turn toward the footsteps coming our way.

I tense.

I've never actually met Max Emory, but I've heard he's... extremely out there. As in, he has a pet gecko in his office rather than a fish. Keeps goats randomly on hotel property, actually has a foundation for them now called Hades and Persephone Farms, and well, the list goes on and on.

And on.

Some people say he even thinks of himself as a matchmaker of sorts in his spare time, but they also say in that same sentence that he nearly killed the last two interns he promoted, so who knows?

You'd think that would deter anyone from working for his massive empire, but the pay is really good for an intern; plus, you smack that on one of your resumes, and people are impressed you actually survived Hadesgate.

Whatever that is.

I mean, I've heard rumors that the goat attacked an employee, but I'm sure that's all just office gossip.

He turns the corner, dressed in a smart navy blue suit with his chocolate hair slicked back. His strong jaw is shockingly attractive, as are his eyes. Actually, if I was into men in their late thirties, I'd say he was sexy.

He stops and crosses his arms, staring all of us down. The entire office is completely silent. I'm afraid to swallow because it might make a noise.

Am I breathing too loud?

Oh no! He glances my way, then quickly averts his eyes.

I breathe a silent sigh of relief.

"The second annual Emory Games are about to begin," he announces in a boisterous voice. "This year, however, will be a little different."

What the hell are the Emory Games?

But also, does this include Hadesgate?

"I'm sure you're wondering what the hell the Emory Games

are…" He grins. "Follow me." He suddenly stops; I nearly run into his back before he turns around and adds, "Don't walk loud; it irritates the gecko."

And that, folks, was my first intro into what would soon be—the weirdest few weeks of my life.

CHAPTER *Two*

Jack

I don't hate her.

I think she *thinks* I hate her.

It's more of a: I have a really hard time tolerating her holier-than-thou attitude, and that's constant.

Would it kill her to have one hair out of place? Roll around in some dirt? I swear I sometimes look back on the one moment we had, and she actually sneered at me when she got too close like I was this complete waste of time.

I grabbed the first girl I could find and swore I'd never let *her* get under my skin again, no matter how pretty she was or how much she wanted to strangle me.

It was really all we had between us.

An immense amount of tension that sometimes felt sexual if I were being completely honest.

Damn, I wonder if she'd freak out if I just threw her

against that conference table and tugged those thick nylons down with my teeth, forcing her to walk around with holes in them the rest of the day.

Yeah, weird fantasy, and yet I'm still getting hard as I try to walk quietly behind the rest of the interns. What the hell does he mean "loud walking upsets the gecko"?

Are lizards that sensitive to noise?

And isn't his office above us, not below?

Jude elbows me. I don't know him well, but he has inky black hair and really blue eyes, which pretty much means every girl in the office flirts with him, including the cougars. "Who do you think he's going to pair you with?"

"Pair me?" I frown. "What do you mean?"

He rolls his eyes. "Come on, bro, The Emory Games. The. Emory. Games!"

Why does he say it twice? And why the hell is he raising his hands like he's auditioning for The Godfather?

He shakes his head like I'm the dumb one. "Why else would you apply for this internship? It went viral last year, the shit he put his interns through just to win a bonus plus a guaranteed job in management. It's literally the only reason people apply for this job now. We probably had to beat out at least two thousand other applicants."

I'm in shock.

I had no idea.

I just thought it sounded like a good way to get out of law school and get my dad off my back about taking my LSATs.

I'm still confused when we all find seats in a theater-like room with cushy leather chairs and a giant screen up front.

"Lights, please." Max claps his hands and moves to the side.

The smell of popcorn fills the air.

But, seriously, what the hell?

Suddenly, honest to God, I'm getting handed popcorn and a soda while the screen flickers then lights up with "A Max Emory Production" during work hours, so, whatever... I'll eat. I'll drink. I'll play.

Music plays.

And then hell ensues as I watch teams of two go through challenge courses and weird gameshow shit.

The music slowly shifts to something more romantic as the camera pans in on an apartment with two of the interns. They're arguing, trapped in a closet, sweaty, then building a bed, and then sleeping in it, and oh shit.

That would make a Hollywood scene look bad.

Is this fucking legal?

The scene fades to black.

The pair is outside competing again. They lose, but they somehow win. I can't tell what happens except everyone's cheering for them even though they were in last place.

Words scroll across the screen; my eyes widen as I read.

"Each winning contestant was given a ten thousand dollar signing bonus along with a job at Emory Enterprises starting at eighty thousand a year, a company car, and a company penthouse apartment."

Sign me the fuck up!

I nearly jump to my feet, throw my hands into the air, and yell, "I volunteer as tribute!"

I still live with my parents.

But for real, I'll kiss that damn gecko if that's what it takes, and lizards scare the shit out of me. It's their eyes like they know things.

All the things.

Adrenaline courses through me as I look around the room. I have at least twenty pounds of muscle on most guys here, the girls look anything but athletic, plus I played collegiate level sports.

I'm going to destroy them all!

I wonder if we get to choose partners.

I start eyeing all the girls and get irritated when I realize that my best prospect would actually be my greatest enemy.

Ivy.

She played volleyball in college and was actually pretty good. She also did gymnastics in high school, not that I actually paid much attention.

Really, I didn't. I mean, cool, you can do the splits and are super bendy, and that does not, at all, lead me to think about things we can do in bed.

I gulp. Ever.

She has an athletic body and would honestly be my only ticket to the top.

Damn it!

Why did we have to argue this morning?

Fucking staples.

"Now," Max says as a crafty grin spreads across his face. "I'll give you a second to digest the movie you just witnessed. This year, as I said, we will be doing things a bit different. First things first, you're going to be allowed to choose your own partner since last time we paired people up, we almost had babies *ha-ha*, am I right?"

He holds his hand up for a high five to his assistant Dustin, whose eyes are twitching behind his black-rimmed glasses as he rocks back and forth and whispers, "We're going to get sued again."

I choke on my laugh.

"Nonsense." Max smacks him on the back. The poor guy's glasses come flying off. "That was one time."

"That was last week," he says through grit teeth.

"Dustin, Dustin, Dustin…" Max chuckles. "You'll scare the littles." He lowers his voice. "Look at their brains, like little gerbils running in their little cages on those circle things; what are they called again?"

"Wheels—"

"Never mind, I'm bored now. Did you start those dance lessons I asked you to?"

Dustin shakes his head.

I notice people start to get up like they're going to pair up the way you would when working on a group project, so I do what any desperate guy does: I jump the seats and plop down next to Ivy with a grunt.

She jumps in response and leans so far away from me that I wonder if she's going to fall on the floor. "Can I help you?"

"We can help each other," I say. "Look, hear me out. I know you hate me, and I hate you, blah, blah, sorry for the staples, but…" I hold out my hands. "We would destroy the competition. We're athletes in our prime, just graduated college. It's not like we're forty."

Max clears his throat.

"Not that there is anything wrong with that," I say loud enough for him and everyone else to hear.

"Better." Max sniffs.

"Anyway…" I lower my voice. "If we get to choose our own partners, we're each other's best bet. Did you see what the winners get? That's huge!"

Her eyes narrow. "But you're rich?"

"And that automatically makes everything perfect?" I scowl. "The last thing I want is to work for my father and be stuck living at home until I'm forty!"

Max clears his throat again.

"Not that there is anything wrong with a finely dressed man in his prime!" I nearly yell it this time.

Max adjusts his tie and smiles. "I am, aren't I?"

"Yes, sir," Dustin answers so quick my head spins a bit.

"Wasn't speaking to you," Max snaps, then rolls his eyes. "Family, can't live with them, can't live without them. Then you end up hiring your cousin because your aunt has gout, and look at me now…"

"Still in your prime, sir," Dustin says through clenched teeth.

I shake my head and look back to Ivy. Her brown eyes are studying me. She tucks her hair behind her ears and continues to stare. Shit, is she even breathing at this point?

She looks down at her clenched hands in her lap. "You do have a bit of a point."

"Is that your way of saying I'm right?"

"Maybe." She refuses to make eye contact and squirms in her seat; it's kind of cute.

Wait, no, not at all, it's hateful and immature, and girls are gross.

Fuck, what the hell is wrong with me?

She leans in. "What do I get out of this?"

"Um, a job?" Is she dense? "A bonus? Take your pick!"

She holds out her hand.

I reach for it, only for her to pull it back.

"I'm confused," I say.

"I'll shake on it, but I want something from you." She leans in.

Her lips are shiny. Normally lip gloss scares me; so many ways that a kiss can taste horrible or go wrong, but hers is pink, and her tongue sneaks out to lick her bottom lip. I'm a bit too entranced when she snaps her fingers in front of me.

"Will you give it to me?"

Wait, what did she just ask me?

"Give it?" I repeat.

She leans in farther—shit, is it a billion degrees in the room? I lean in too.

Her mouth is so close to mine that it would take maybe another ten inches, and I could seal our deal with a really work-appropriate kiss, you know, like the Europeans do, right? That's a thing. I saw a documentary about it once.

I think.

Why am I thinking about kissing?

She thinks I hate her. Maybe I do. Maybe I hate that I like her. So basically, I hate myself.

Focus on the hate, not the lip gloss.

"I want…" she starts.

Please say my cock, please say my cock.

Son of a bitch, has it really been that long? Am I that desperate?

Calm the hell down!

"Your stapler." She pulls back and crosses her arm. "And you have to promise not to buy another one, no more stapling!"

I snort out a laugh. "Damn, put a pencil behind your ear and add some glasses, and you'd be the teacher of my dreams."

Her cheeks flare bright red.

Hmmm, does she like that?

She ignores me. "So, do we have a deal?"

Damn it, I really like driving her crazy. I hold out my hand anyway and say, "Deal."

"I'll expect it on my desk by five." She grins like she just won the lottery, and I'm still stuck on the whole turning in my stapler to her desk teacher scenario.

I really need to get myself under control if I'm going to be her partner.

We shake hands, and that's it. I have a new partner in crime. I exhale a sigh of relief and turn to see that most everyone else is paired up as well.

"Great!" Max claps his hands. "Looks like most of you found someone you can tolerate the competitions with. Now for the information on this year's Emory Games!"

The lights lower again.

I'm pumped.

I would love to do a ninja course or something like that.

I'm giddy with excitement when the first picture comes up.

Market Research.

Huh?

"Love abounds." Max spreads his arms wide. "This year, Emory Hotels has purchased a company that produces dating manuals, soaps, lotions, and various products that help the younger generation date more efficiently since so many people are choosing online dating efficiency is everything. Because of the sensitivity of the product, we've had HR come up with a few different tests for you to do as a pair. We don't want to get sued again," he says with laughs.

I'm so still now, I'm the one not breathing.

"You'll be living across the hall from each other, we couldn't swing the whole roommate thing again, but you will be spending the next two weeks together as if you're…"

Don't say it. Don't say it. Don't say it.

"Dating."

"Fuck!" I say, then realize I said it out loud.

When a heel drives into the top of my foot seconds later.

CHAPTER
Three

Ivy

I'm so embarrassed I want to cry.

I hold the tears in the entire meeting, and when we break for the rest of the day and go to our desks, I'm surprised to see the stapler already there with a note on top that says sorry.

Yeah right, he's just sorry he picked me.

Could this *get* any worse?

"Too bad." Jude stops by my desk and leans over it. "I would have loved to fake date you for two weeks."

He smells so good.

Damn it! Jude? I could have fake-dated Jude instead of the devil? Where is the recount? HUH?! FAKE NEWS! I demand a re-do!

I'm the one that said yes, though.

See! Just another way Jack is RUINING my life.

I slam my hand down on the stapler, a lone staple comes tumbling out like it's mocking me. I take a deep breath. "That would have been fun."

"Maybe another time." He winks. "We can't fake date, but..." He shrugs. "We could always—"

"Stop trying to manipulate my partner," Jack snaps as he comes up behind him. "As of right now, we're in competition, so she's mine, not yours."

Jude gives me a smirk, then wraps his knuckles on my desk. "Knock on wood; you never know what will happen during a competition. May the best man win..." He walks off without looking at Jack.

Jack stares me down like the dad waiting up when you break curfew. "Jude? Really?"

"He's nice." I shrug.

"Nice?" Clearly, I'm exacerbating the situation as he comes around my desk and crowds my space. "My nana is nice, okay? She volunteers for the church, makes casseroles for the homeless, and still watches Wheel of Fortune. That's nice. My old turtle who won't die but just sits there and eats carrots... he's nice. A walk in a field of lilies... that's nice—"

"Did you hit your head?"

"I'm fine!" He raises his voice, then lowers it again. "Jude isn't nice, he's out to win, and he's out to seduce you before I get the chance!"

My stomach erupts with butterflies that need to hurry up and die so I can survive this partnership. "You aren't seducing me; that wasn't part of the rules."

"No, but if it is, then I get to do it as your partner, no your date, you're officially my office date. Deal with it." He seems way angrier than he should be, considering the relationship isn't actually real, but I let it go because, duh, I have his stapler, and it's too weird to even process at this point.

Since when did Jack even care?

Since when did Jude even notice me?

The day can't possibly get weirder—after all, we only have a half-hour left before we get to go home.

I hide a yawn behind my hand when Dustin walks in with a stack of manila envelopes.

He plops them down on our desks.

One has my name on it.

I almost ask if I should open it, but it's not like our bosses hid tarantulas or something in there.

Ha-ha, no but seriously, right?

Then again, Max is super eccentric, but does he really want his interns dying of cardiac arrest?

Negative.

I quickly dump the contents onto my desk.

Inside is a small packet labeled *"Date Number One."*

Next to it is a key.

And finally, directions to my new apartment in the same building I work in. Lovely, now it really is a prison.

I take a deep breath and start to read through the instructions for the first date. Apparently, this company wrote a self-help book on the art of the first date followed by several products that could help guide you into it as well as—oh wow!—as well as after it if you so choose.

The products are already in a basket at each of our apartments. Our job as a team is to plan the perfect in-home first date.

Girls use the products.

Guys have to cook using what's in the fridges.

Must stay for at least two hours and play one of the games created by the company, which helps partners get to know each other.

Great, sounds worse than the stapler!

All teams who make it through the two hours without burning any food, arguing, and learning at least five new facts about one another will be given points—teams must also rate the products and give honest opinions about their effectiveness.

All I keep wondering is why they won't tell us what the products are.

"This is bullshit," Jude says to Anderson. "What does it matter? Isn't this what the R&D team is for?"

Dustin, still standing there, clears his throat. "Max likes to take a more organic approach to research and development. Any product deemed useless won't be sold in any of our stores and will be pulled from all of the company's hotels immediately. Anything given a high score will be rebranded under Emory Enterprises and merchandised. Does that answer your question, boy with waxed eyebrows and a spray tan?"

"I'm Latino, you racist prick," Jude says with a sneer.

"But he does wax his brows, so one for two, Dustin, one for two," Jack adds.

Everyone snickers around us. Jude looks ready to sue, but I know he wants this job just as much as the rest of us.

"Apologies." Dustin turns bright red. "I just—never mind. You have lovely skin. Compliments to your skincare routine; it must take ages to get that dewy look."

"Are you hitting on me now?" Jude asks, his voice laced with shocked disbelief.

Dustin, if possible, turns even more red. "No, no, no, no."

"Damn it, Dustin." Max comes waltzing in. "Do I need to send you to HR again to get the talk?"

"No, sir!" Dustin straightens up.

Max rolls his eyes. "Grow a brain, and while you're at it, do a nice little soul check, would ya?"

"Soul check?" I mouth to Jack.

Jack shakes his head, face twisted and looking as confused as I am.

"Now, do your breathing," Max says to Dustin. "Do you have your rock?"

Dustin breathes in and out in and out while Max pats him on the ass and then looks at us. "Now, only I can do that because he's my cousin, and we've talked about good touch/bad touch; if HR see's any of you doing anything like this, you'll most likely be fired; nice demonstration, though, am I right, Dustin?" He slaps his ass again. "Alrighty." He checks his watch. "You're dismissed. You have exactly twenty minutes to get to your apartments. Clothes have been delivered for you to your exact requirements. If you make a note of what you would like from your dwelling places, we can send someone over to grab things, but you should have all your needs met right down to your shampoo, phone chargers, silk pillowcases, and toothbrushes."

I'm still in shock that we are actually doing this. I feel semi-numb as I grab my stuff and put the contents back into the envelope. I walk into the elevator and see Jude try to make his way over to it.

Jack blocks his way.

And lets himself in, then hits the down button giving Jude a middle finger as the doors close.

I smack him on the chest with my envelope. "Was that necessary?"

"For me?" He snorts out a laugh. "Yes, I can't stand that guy. And for you, double yes, he just wants to fuck you."

"Wow, thank you; what a great way to almost start our first date." Scowling, I turn away from him.

The elevator stops at the company apartment level.

"After you." He holds his hands out as the elevator doors open. You could fit an SUV in the hallway it's so big. From what I can see, there are only four rooms on the floor; mine's to the right, and Jack's is to the left."

"So…" He stops at his door. "Should we just plan on meeting up in an hour or so, just rip that Band-Aid clean off?"

"How romantic," I grumble. "Rip the Band-Aid right off?"

"What?" He shrugs; his hands go to his head as they run through his gorgeous model-like hair. "I'm just saying the sooner we get done, the better, right?"

"Sure, teammate, sure." I want to bang my head against my door. Instead, I call over my shoulder, "Think you can get dinner ready in an hour?"

He mouths it back to me like a toddler, then types in the code to his apartment while I look back at my door and do the same.

His door slams.

Mine follows.

Great start, truly a great start.

I lean against the door and look around. The apartment is super nice, not huge, but I at least have my own bedroom and a bathroom, the ceilings are at least twelve feet, and I have a giant window right in front of my living room that overlooks Lower Manhattan.

Let's be honest, it's probably one of the biggest apartments I've ever been in and could never afford even if I made six figures.

The kitchen is gourmet with whites and grays that make the space feel more open, and the couches match everything perfectly, almost making me want to stay off the couch just in case.

A faux fur rug is draped across the soft white suede couch, and they look so comfy I want to crash.

A flat-screen TV is bolted to the wall, and of course, they have succulents strategically placed around the living area.

I wish I could live here.

But it's temporary, just like dum-dum across the hall—thank God.

I quickly open the card on the table and then stare into the ginormous basket that accompanies it.

I'm expecting perfumes and other products that women use during dates; instead, I'm staring at essential oils for seduction, a dress that looks like it would only fit a toddler, and a few other boxes I'm actually afraid to open.

"You can do this, you can do this," I repeat to myself as I take the tiny black body con dress and pull it up against me. "He's going to see my bits!"

Oh great, now I'm talking to myself.

I drop the dress and pick up the first box. The directions say to add just a bit of the pheromones to my pulse points, and behind my knees-what the hell did I get myself into?

Pheromones?

I shudder and open the next box.

Ah, perfume... perfume I can deal with.

It tells me to spray it on my right wrist and to shake my wrist until the perfume starts to fill the air.

The next card looks daunting, I pick it up, and all it says is. "Get him to seduce you, using the products, your charm, and the dating guide below."

Well, shit did just hit the fan, didn't it?

The dating guide has only four suggestions. "Lean in when he speaks to you, smile as often as you can, use any excuse to lightly touch him, and laugh at everything he says."

Who the hell wrote this? I flip it over and roll my eyes. "From Max Emory's Guide to Dating and Every other Life Question."

He's clinically insane, isn't he?

It's the only explanation.

How does his company even get away with this? Is it some rich person thing? And why do the interns have to test all the products?

I check my phone and realize I only have about forty-five minutes left to make this work. I hope to God that Jack's struggling just as much as I am.

I don't have to wait long as I attempt to pour myself into the black dress, put on some makeup—adding in the oils and weird perfumes, and topping it off with a low bun and the nude heels that were in the box next to the basket.

I add some lip gloss for effect and make my way across the hall; I lift my hand to knock, chicken out, then finally hold my breath as I knock twice.

When the door opens, Jack's standing there completely shirtless. "I can explain."

"Ummm…" I have nothing.

"It burned," he blurts.

"The food?"

"My shirt." He's breathing heavily, and his face is cherry red as he glances around the room. "I mean, the food doesn't look horrible, but the stove wasn't working, and I got too close and—"

I cover my mouth to keep from laughing.

"Not funny." His teeth clench. "I'm half-naked!"

Yeah, he is… " Kind of, though?" I sidestep him just as he leans in and sniffs me.

Wait, is he actually sniffing my neck?

He jerks back like he realizes what he just did, then scratches the back of his head, showing off some impressive abs and smooth skin, plus one large tattoo that goes down his right side.

"A dragon?" I point at it.

"They're fierce, and I wanted to piss my dad off, so I found the biggest one I could do with my pain tolerance and went for it." He winks and walks over to the stove.

The table is set.

A bottle of wine sits in the middle, already opened, and both glasses are poured like a real date.

He even has the white linen tablecloth on correctly.

A single red rose lays across my plate.

Hmm, maybe it won't be so bad…

"Shit! Fuck! Motherfucking chicken!" Jack shouts.

I nearly break an ankle as I rush over to see that he's burned one side and is on his way to burning the other which means no points for us unless I step in. "Let me help."

"I've got this." He jerks away from me.

"No, you burned an actual shirt from your body. Jack, that doesn't scream I've got this; that screams fire department and burning down an entire office building!"

"I can do it." He takes a deep breath. "So how was, um, getting ready in that thing you call a dress."

"Ah, this old thing?" I lean against the counter. "Let's just say I almost had to open it up with scissors, turn it into a scarf, and walk in here half-naked."

He drops the spatula and picks it up again. "And that would be bad because...?"

"Ew!" I smack him. "You barely know me."

"Correction." He points the spatula at me. "I've known you since middle school. We just never ran in the same circles."

"Rich people circles."

"Oh no, I meant popular people circles." He winks.

I want to wrap my dress around his neck and squeeze.

"You look nice, though," he says. "And I say that as your partner."

I strut over to the table and grab my glass of wine. "Hope you have more of this because I'm about ready to slam this entire bottle."

"Be my guest." He keeps cooking or attempting to cook. The oven goes off, and half-naked Jack grabs his oven mitts and pulls out fresh bread. He also has the salad already made and on the table and what looks like fresh asparagus in the oven with the bread.

"Smells good." I sip the wine. It's clearly expensive. I check out the label and sigh. "Emory Wines?" I hold it up. "Is everything an Emory product?"

"Even my spatula." Jack holds it up. "It's insane. The guy tries to market everything. Probably why he's rich."

"Probably why he can afford to put us through hell to test all of his new products without paying a few six-figure sums to the R&D team."

Jack snorts. "I think he just likes torture."

"That too." I toss back more wine and suddenly start to get hot. Maybe the alcohol is getting to me? I ate today, though, and half a glass shouldn't really do much to me.

I start to fan myself. My cheeks are heating, and something

starts to pulse down my neck—down my body, actually. What the hell?

Jack turns off the stove and starts plating all the food. When he's done, he brings the plates over and sets them on the table, then freezes and looks over at me. "What are you wearing?"

"A dress?"

"Not the damn dress." He swallows slowly; his eyes dilate as he takes a step toward me and inhales. "What perfume are you wearing?"

"What they put in the basket, why?"

"No, it's not even—" He gets closer, crowding me against the counter. "It smells like candy, but the good kind you could lick and lick and lick and—" He stops himself again. "Is this a trick?"

"Is what a trick? God, I'm so hot I could take my entire dress off. Isn't it hot in here? It feels hot!" I start fanning myself.

He starts taking labored breaths.

I don't know who reaches out first, but suddenly I'm in his arms, and he's staring at my mouth like he wants to participate in the licking, not the eating of dinner.

I gulp. "I think it's the pheromones."

"You put on pheromones!"

"It was part of my task!"

"THEN UNTASK IT!" he yells. "Untask it *right* the hell now!" He lets out a moan. "Fuck... you smell good."

"Let's just eat the chicken," I say in a shaky voice.

He stumbles back and pulls out my chair. It topples over twice before he gets it to stay. He goes for his and sits so close to the edge he nearly falls onto the floor. Then he continues to Edward Cullen vampire stare at me for the next five minutes before he apparently realizes what he's been doing. "Sorry."

"I smell. I know."

His voice is raspy, needy. "So much better than my burned chicken."

"Hey, you at least cooked it!" Too well, but I didn't add that.

"So, any other surprises?" he asks, giving me a suspicious, one-eye-narrowed stare.

I choke on my wine.

"Oh no, let me have it."

"I just have to get you to do something for me..."

"What?" The sound of silverware scraping the plates fills the room as I keep the task to myself because isn't this weird? Wrong?

"Never mind." I drink more.

I eat to settle my stomach.

And my annoyance.

I yawn after we finish eating, only to have him bring out dessert from the fridge. It's a gorgeous tiramisu that I know he didn't make.

"The only thing not burned," I comment.

Jack makes a face. "Very funny."

He's still shirtless, and it's impossible not to stare.

I reach for my fork, but he presses his hand over mine and shakes his head, "You aren't the only one with a task."

"Wh-what?"

"Come here." He crooks his finger. "I'm going to feed you now."

I hand him my fork.

He sighs and hangs his head again. "Nah, with my finger."

Well damn.

I wasn't ready.

Max woke up and chose violence, didn't he?

Are there hidden cameras?

What do I even do right now?

I lean forward. "This can't be legal."

"It's probably in our NDAs." Jack licks his lips, then stares at mine as he dips his finger into the tiramisu and holds it out to my mouth.

Well, here we go!

My first mistake was going with it.

My second comes when I lean forward and hear a small rip come from my ass.

"What was that?" he asks with a smirk.

I'm not even kidding when I almost say I farted just to save myself from admitting the dress is too small and my ass is too big.

I quickly lick his finger and say, "Mmmmmm, so gooooooood! Give me more!"

The distraction works as he quickly dips his finger into the tiramisu. I eat more and wonder how I'm going to walk backward toward that door.

The cake is almost done.

And I have zero time.

I keep eating.

Thinking.

Third mistake is being distracted as Jack leans forward with a smile. I think he's going to actually kiss me when he turns my head to the side and looks over my shoulder. "Knew you'd have a nice ass."

I sucker punch him in the stomach.

It was instinct!

He starts coughing and falls to the floor, yelling, "Whyyyyyyy?" like I just committed murder.

Whatever.

I kick him lightly. "You're fine; stop being dramatic!"

"It was a compliment!" He slowly gets to his feet. "Who taught you to hit?"

"My grandma."

He laughs, then stops. "Oh shit, seriously? Was she like a Kung Fu master or something?"

"She got bored easy and started taking karate, then Kung Fu, Jiu-Jitsu, Krav Maga—she got around."

"Yeah, she did. I think I'd like to meet her." He smiles and stands to his feet.

And my heart sinks.

"She's…" I can't say it; saying it makes me feel like I'm manifesting it even more, and I'm still not over losing my best friend. "Anyway, thanks for the cake and date; I'll just head back to my side of the building."

"Hey." Jack reaches for my hand. "I'm sorry. I didn't know."

"How could you? We're strangers, remember? Sworn enemies and all that."

"Yeah." He leans in. His nose is cold as it presses against my neck. "Sworn enemies… that's what this feeling is."

"It's the perfume."

"And the ass," he adds.

I smack him again, then hold the material together in the back as he opens the door, and I shuffle across the hall and into my apartment.

It takes me a while to sleep. And when it does finally come—I think of my grandma, and then I imagine her meeting Jack.

And I smile.

CHAPTER
Four

Jack

'm exhausted.

Sleep is impossible.

All I keep seeing is *her* ass, then thinking of a grandma kicking *my* ass, then about how good Ivy smells... and yeah, it was a night.

I wake up to a package at my door and a text. I grab the package after reading the text that instructs me to put on the clothes and meet downstairs at noon.

Ivy opens her door the minute I start to close mine. Her box is identical. Huh.

"Did you have a good—"

She shuts the door before I can finish.

Whatever.

We aren't together for real; this is all fake, fake, fake dating. Fun, so fun.

I need to just focus on the potential bonus and job opportunities before I do something stupid like kiss her—which I almost did last night until her dress ripped, then almost did again when she left.

What the hell is wrong with me?

I quickly get dressed in this weird black tracksuit that looks like I'm ready to go for a run but with an old guy who works for the mafia, wears a gold chain, and has a rasp in his voice.

I leave the apartment at the same time Ivy does. She's wearing a matching tracksuit, which makes things get weirder.

Jude's waiting by the elevator when we get on, his partner nowhere to be seen; he also isn't wearing the tracksuit. "Stupid competition."

"What happened?" Ivy asks.

He rolls his eyes. "I had two tasks, and my fake date freaked out! I kissed her. I mean, it's not like I forced her, she came on to me! But—"

"Fake or not, you never attempt that, bro," I say. "Read the room. *You* probably freaked her out if you got all into it."

"This is stupid anyway," Jude says once we get in.

Ivy steps closer to me, and I kind of like it; I like that she's putting distance and air between her and that dick.

Maybe now she gets the whole arrogant vibe from him like I do, the one that says nobody is good enough for him, but he'll take it because he just likes to use women.

We say nothing to each other as we get off the elevator and meet in the lobby; Jude keeps walking. I wonder if he got fired.

The rest of the interns are down here wearing various colors of tracksuits. It's so strange?

Dustin's waiting in his typical bowtie and black-rimmed glasses; he's carrying an iPad and grinning from ear to ear.

"Welcome to day two of The Emory Games. I have to be completely honest; we had to test everyone yesterday to see if you would truly follow through with our instructions. Our safety measures are different this year, so you understand why we would do that; today will be much different."

I breathe a sigh of relief.

He clears his throat. "We've eliminated one couple already; sadly, Brad and Jessie are gone. The rest of you will be competing for the next few days in a brand-new game that has nothing to do with seduction or our products. Count yourselves lucky because Max just bought this company called Passion Plus, and they have the hugest dil—"

"And that's where you learn to stop talking," Max says as he walks up and slaps Dustin on the back, making his glasses go askew on his face. "But as he said, welcome to day two. Now," he says as he checks his watch, "let's get going." He rubs his hands together after that like he's gleefully pumped to be at work right now.

Which only means one thing.

We should have all just gone along with seduction and pheromones.

I grab Ivy's hand and pull her back. "Tell me you're not terrified."

She rolls her eyes. "What could be worse than last night?"

"EXACTLY my thoughts," I hiss. "Imagine!"

"You worry too much, oh stapler of blank paper. We'll be fine."

I gulp. "Okay."

"Everyone in the vans!" Max claps.

In hindsight, I was right, she was wrong. I will one day make T-shirts to commemorate the rare moment.

The trip takes about an hour.

There's this huge building a bit outside of Manhattan that looks like it was once a hotel or laser tag sort of place. It says Escape Room ETC.

Huh, I've kind of always wanted to do one of those.

I'm feeling more confident.

And then Max lets us in the building and locks the door behind us. "Dustin, will you please start the cameras for our guests?" He adjusts his tie.

"Guests?" I ask.

"Oh, yes!" Max nods eagerly. "We always allow our Board of Directors to watch The Emory Games. It invigorates their old souls." And just like that, Max opens a black door and goes up a few stairs.

It shuts with finality along with Dustin's mouth as he smiles weakly at us and points to another black door. "Just through there, instructions will come over the loudspeaker." He starts to walk away, then backs up and says, "You've all signed your NDAs, correct?"

Ummmmm.

Nods go around.

I want to yell no.

I want to grab the door, but it closes as he escapes through it.

"Open it," I tell Ivy.

"You open it!" she says back.

Anderson sighs. "Guys, for once, could you just not argue?"

Grumbling goes around the rest of the interns as he pulls open the door.

It's super dark inside the room.

If this is a haunted house, I am officially out.

I'm scared of the dark the way I'm scared of lizards.

The lights flicker on.

And all I can say is I'm stunned shitless. A life-sized version of Max Emory dressed as this girl in an orange dress is facing away from us. When I glance around, I realize it's a legit exact replica of Squid Game, where the contestants would play their first game, red light, green light. If you get caught by the giant girl or Max, you get fucking shot. And you still have to make it past the finish line in minutes.

"IS HE MURDERING US?" someone yells.

"We're a Dateline episode."

"I sucked at this game as a kid!" People start yelling and running in all directions like we're about to get bombed or something.

Music starts.

And then his voice, like that of the devil, comes over the loudspeaker. "Make it across the line in two minutes. If big Maxine sees you move, you're toast."

"I hate toast," I whisper, suddenly clutching Ivy by the arm. "It's so dry. I really hate it."

Ivy shrugs away. "Man up! We can do this. We just have to go fast and then freeze like we did as kids during freeze tag."

Easy? EASY?

"Which part of running with a different crowd did you not understand?" I hiss. "I never played freeze tag! I played basketball!"

She grins at me; it's cute, but I know the horror behind that grin and what it means. "Then you're dead."

"How are you so cruel?" I cling to her. "Who hurt you?"

She shoves me off her. "Oh, some big giant idiot in college, but I'm over it."

"I'm not," I say under my breath, making her own catch. Does fear cause a person to just blurt shit out like that? What the hell is wrong with me?

"Three," Max's voice comes over the loudspeaker.

I'm not ready.

"Two."

"SHIT!" I yell. "Help!"

Ivy grabs me by the arm and holds me behind her.

"One!"

We're still as the music plays, and "Maxine" turns around and then turns back. Another couple trips next to us, and shots ring out.

From a paintball gun.

I'm still not relieved because that shit hurts.

Maxine turns back around.

"Run!" Ivy shoves me forward. She doesn't have to tell me twice. I sprint toward the line, then stop and topple over onto my knees. When Maxine turns back around, I'm as still as I can be.

I don't get shot.

I can feel Ivy behind me.

She helps me up, and we make it across in record time, but my heart is still slamming against my chest.

Ivy falls to the ground next to me. "That was intense."

"That was insane," I grumble. "I mean, it's just paintball, but still."

She holds her hand up for a high five. "You did it!"

"Yeah, well, I have a super good partner." I nudge her.

She laughs.

And I realize I'm probably in more trouble right now than I was last night.

Shit.

CHAPTER
Five

Max

"**Y**ou see, Dustin, the thing about loyal employees... they're willing to do just about anything for money or a stable job. The economy's rough, as you well know, considering the shoes you choose to wear." Max beams at the row of board members around him. "Thank you all for coming!"

Dustin grumbles something under his breath.

"What was that, little D?" Max asks, cupping his ear.

"Little D?" Roger, one of the younger board members with perfectly slicked back black hair, an impeccable gray suit, and shiny black shoes, asks.

"I'm glad you said something, Roger; thank you. Your voice soothes the soul." Max puts his hands together in front of him. "It was a nickname from childhood after a girl told him he had a small—"

"We should probably get started!" Dustin all but yells, then coughs wildly into his hands.

Max sighs. "Fun ruiner."

Dustin shoots him a glare. "If you'll just bring your attention to the player board and place your bets, we'll be sure to get them into the system before the next event."

Roger pipes up again, "Can we bet on them all?"

"No." Max wags his finger at Roger. "You know you have to pick only one. That's why it's important to study the player profiles thoroughly. You pick one team, and if they win, then you win the entire pot of cash plus bragging rights. Everyone else, however…" Max grins. "Will have their names added to the trophy of shame and donate a pre-determined amount to the charity of their choice." He rolls his eyes. "And people think this is cruel. You know we single-handedly saved the Penguin Palace at the zoo last year because of the Emory Games?"

Max puffs out his chest. "Now, grab your avatar, and place your bets. I naturally won't be betting since I have insider information. There are currently eight active board members, and each of you has picked something that represents you in some way. Roger, you chose an owl. Dane, I noticed you grabbed a lizard, which makes sense, all things considered."

Dane, is, in fact, wearing head-to-toe green but shrugs as if he isn't aware that he looks, in fact, exactly like a lizard.

"Now." Max rubs his hands together. "There are only a few left to pick from." He steps away and points at the smart board.

Each team is labeled team one, two, three, four, and so on; each of them have different colors matching their team, and the setup looks like a virtual horse race.

"Currently, the team favored to win is Ivy and Jack, team

number two, but I wouldn't discount some of the others. It's easy to come out fists flying; it's hard to finish first when you start first. Just ask Dustin."

"I was in high school, and I tripped on a shoelace." Dustin glares from behind his black-rimmed glasses.

"There, there." Max pats him on the shoulder. "We all, at some point in life, trip on the finish line and choke during the state finals." He slaps Dustin hard on the back again. "All right, now, time to announce the next game!"

Cheers erupted around the boardroom as everyone scrambles to place their bets on the large board on the giant conference table.

Max grins to himself.

Look at that. Creating a fantastic company climate, one bet at a time!

CHAPTER
Six

Ivy

'm terrified of what the morning is going to bring. After the trauma of paintball, I've developed insomnia. Whenever I close my eyes, I see Maxine turning and staring at me.

Just staring.

A creepy smile almost always emerges.

She doesn't blink.

Somehow a lizard shows up, don't ask me why, and that's it, you know, other than thinking about the devil across the hall.

I want to get up and see if he wants to watch Netflix or something since we don't have to actually report to our next game until noon, but I feel weird.

After today, when he showed how vulnerable he really could be during the game and then somehow confessed he wasn't over whatever moment we had, I've been feeling strange.

My stomach is unsettled.

I feel like I can't catch my breath.

And I think about him way too much while I'm lying there staring up at the ceiling.

I punch the pillow with my right hand and then scream into it. A sudden knock sounds on my door. I'm ashamed of how fast I jump out of bed and sprint toward the door in nothing but my white silk sleep shorts and nearly see-through white top. I quickly grab one of the puffy black coats I had lying on the chair and put it on.

I take a deep breath and open the door.

There he is.

The man of both dreams and nightmare, leaning against the doorframe like he has a right to look this sexy when yesterday he was hiding behind me and using me as a human shield.

"You," I say, voice low.

"Me." He walks right in without my permission and shuts the door behind him.

I back up a few steps, confused.

He stops short and narrows his eyes on me. "You cold?"

Actually, no, now I'm sweating bullets. But I lie. "Yeah, freezing."

"So, you didn't think to grab a blanket instead of a winter coat?" He smirks.

Damn him.

"It's a personal preference thing." I lift my chin.

"It's huge." He flicks my puffy arm and walks past me. "Couldn't sleep, thought we could hang out. I'm bored out of my mind, and every time I close my eyes, I see Maxine." He shudders.

I laugh. "Yeah, same here; it's like he knew it would imprint on our souls."

"Should have never taken that internship." He winks.

Warmth spreads through my body. "Well, it was the only place that paid well."

"And now we know why." He grabs the remote and points it at me. "What do you feel like watching?"

"What makes you think I want to watch anything with you?"

He looks away, so confident I want to smack him in the head. "You do."

I'm already walking toward him, my legs betraying me before my mind can tell them to run in the opposite direction and lock the door to the master bedroom.

I sit down on the couch, putting space between us while he clicks on Netflix and starts some creepy crime documentary about neighbors and squatters.

I'm sweating even harder.

I need to take off the jacket.

I'm so uncomfortable an hour in that I can't stop moving on the couch.

Finally, Jack pauses the documentary, turns to me, and runs a hand through his hair, looking way too sexy. "Take it off."

If anything, I hold the jacket tighter. "Excuse me?"

"Your jacket. You're driving me crazy; you're so stubborn! Just take it off and relax; it's not like I'm going to suddenly hump you on the couch or anything because I see skin. Even I have self-control."

I snort. "Sure you do."

He puts the remote down and gets up, then walks over to me, pulls me to my feet, shoves my hands down, and unzips the jacket in one fluid movement that has it opening right up to him.

Revealing perky breasts, all the see-thoroughness, and my sweaty skin.

His eyes drink me in before he clears his throat and looks

away, stumbling backward. "See? Totally fine."

He looks anything but.

I do like his reaction, though.

I like that he seems off balance.

So, I drop the jacket to the floor and sit back down on the couch.

"Do you, uh…" He scratches the back of his head. "Need like a blanket? Or a pillow? Something to hug, you know, since it's a scary… documentary?"

I shrug. "Nah, I'm good."

"Ha-ha." His laugh is so obviously fake. "Yeah, same, same, was just thinking that too. Maybe I'll just get one, though, in case I get cold."

He jerks a throw blanket out from under the coffee table and places it across his lap. I scoot closer to him. He has nowhere to go. And I'm pretty sure I know what he's hiding under that blanket.

He scratches his head, runs his hands through his hair again, then folds his hands in his lap.

Less than five minutes later, he grabs a pillow.

"Are you okay?" I ask. "Now, you're the fidgety one."

"Yeah, totally fine." He doesn't look at me.

I'm very much reminded of the rejection. The hurt. I scoot even closer. He completely stills, his jaw clenches.

I've always noticed his jaw.

I've always noticed *him*.

I think that's where the hate started, with knowing that he's never really noticed me in the same way, and I refuse to count the stapling.

He inhales and exhales, slowly, like he's afraid to breathe

Do I smell?

I tuck my feet under my body and cross my arms.

He lets out a little groan.

"Seriously." I give him a shove. "What's with you?"

"You really, really, really…" He turns to his left, then looks back at the TV immediately. "…*really* need to grab a blanket. A sweater. A parka. Put the damn down puffy jacket back on. Or I heard muumuus are in again."

I frown. "But I'm not cold; you're being weird."

"No, you're hot," he says almost to himself. "So hot, I'm hot too, a different kind of hot."

"Then take off the blanket." I reach for it.

"No!" He grabs my hands while I'm trying to pull the blanket off his lap, and then I'm suddenly falling forward right on top of him, only a blanket and his thin black T-shirt blocking our skin from touching.

He's hot.

His eyes flicker to my lips. "Question."

"What now?"

"If I kiss you, will you slap me?"

I grin. "This sounds like a fun game."

"Be serious."

"I am." I lean in. "Care to test it out?"

"How hard do you slap?"

"How good do you kiss?"

He smirks. "Ah, a challenge?"

"I like to win."

"Maybe we both win…"

I lean closer, our faces barely a foot apart at this point. "So, kissing you is the equivalent to winning?"

He swallows slowly, tucking my hair behind my ears. "Even if it was like losing to me, I'd probably still do it."

"Brutal honesty, Mr. Self-control."

His eyes soften, and determination follows as he grips me by the back of the neck and pulls me in for a kiss. It's perfect timing. I'm shocked, so my lips part. He devours my moan; his tongue massages mine gently. I squeak as his hands find my ass and grip it.

I need to feel him.

Now.

I try to pull the blanket out from between us. His hands help my frantic movements, he lifts me momentarily, and then the blanket's on the floor, and I'm nearly naked on top of him, my silk shorts basically hide nothing, and my nipples harden against his chest.

He curses against my mouth and deepens the kiss.

I pull back and lift my hand.

His eyes widen as if to say are you serious?

"Kidding." I wink. "I just wanted to scare you."

"Yes, because slapping won't kill the moment." He grips my wrists. I writhe against him because now I really do wanna give him a light smack.

That might be fun.

I keep squirming.

He bites down on his lower lip. "I'm embarrassed to admit this, but if you don't stop moving around on top of me, I'm going to do something I haven't done since middle school."

"Have sex?" I ask. "You little whore."

He glares. "Very funny."

I burst out laughing, stop moving, and lean down to kiss him again; he flips me onto my back.

I have no idea what I'm doing. In the morning, I'm going to regret doing this with my partner, but I can't stop.

And I can feel he doesn't want to either.

Maybe it's just adrenaline from earlier today.

We're young.

We're enemies.

But we still have needs. Right?

I moan, and he abruptly pulls back and stands. There's no mistaking the way he feels, and he doesn't even try to hide his arousal as he stretches his arms above his head. "Wow, it's getting late; I should, you know... go."

I'm half on the couch, half on the floor staring up at him, completely ready to keep making out; my heart's pounding, and he's just talking about how late it is?

"Wow." I stand. "Guess some things never change."

He doesn't meet my eyes. "Yeah, guess so."

"Once a player, always a player?" I snort. "Glad I was convenient for your insomnia."

"Yeah," he snaps. "I feel so much fucking better now; thanks for the make-out session; it was one hundred percent what I needed, even better than counting sheep or meditating, put me right out."

He actually yawns.

I stomp toward him.

He stumbles back and walks to the door.

I'm going to murder him.

He opens it and then hesitates while I'm looking for a sharp object to throw at him. Is this just his thing? Kiss me? Make me want him? Then leave? At least this time he's not going to find some random girl in the hallway.

I follow him just in case... without a sharp weapon, though I'm ready to scratch anyone's eyes out, don't ask me why.

I feel violent.

Hurt.

Embarrassed.

Was the kiss bad?

Was it because I kissed him back?

I have too many questions, and I hate that he always leaves me with those questions and annoyance.

And oftentimes embarrassment that I did something wrong. Maybe I'm the shiny thing he's tempted to grab only to realize it's tarnished when he gets up close.

I self-consciously tuck my hair back when he sighs and continues opening the door. He walks across the hall, scans his card over his door, and opens it.

I look down the hallway.

It's empty.

"I'm sorry." He looks over his shoulder at me. "That wasn't why I came over. I'm—just, I'm sorry."

"That's what every girl wants to hear after getting kissed." I glare. "That you're sorry it happened."

"That's not what I said—"

I slam my door and slide to the carpeting. This really can't happen again. I won't make it through without committing murder, and I'm too young for prison. What is with him? It's not like we're friends crossing a line. We're enemies trying to survive, who happen to kiss like the world's on fire.

My head falls back against the door in a slow *thunk*. "Whatever," I say to myself and get up, then look over at the couch. The blanket's on the floor.

The documentary is still on.

And I wish he was still there too.

Something's wrong with me because I'm falling for him all over again, and all he did was kiss me and remind me why I fell for him in the first place.

How easy it was to be with him, how fun and entertaining it was to throw him off his game, how great it was to challenge him.

But now I have nothing.

I turn off the lights in the living room and make my way toward the master. Sleep doesn't find me for a long time. When I close my eyes, I see his smile and feel his kiss.

And I hate him all over again.

Damn stapler.

CHAPTER
Seven

Jack

'm an idiot.

The biggest idiot in the world.

I throw a pillow over my face and wonder if it would be better if someone just held it down and put me out of my misery.

I've never been pissed about having a good memory until this moment. I brushed my teeth seven times last night and still tasted her—it was so damn good that I want to curse.

The way she moved against me was so erotically painful that I wondered if I should just rip the shorts from her body and say fuck it.

But it was hormones, right?

I mean, I like her, she makes me laugh, and she's annoyingly pretty and annoying all at once, but a one-night stand with my partner, the other intern, just sounds like the worst idea ever, even though my body was like yes, best idea, do it, do it, we want it.

And now I'm hard again.

I jump out of bed and awkwardly walk with a baseball bat between my legs toward the shower. When I get there, I stare down at my dick and almost hear it say, oh hey there, was getting ready for a fun night. You suck. I like her. Eat shit.

"Cold it is." I turn it as cold as possible, jump in, and curse her all over again.

It wouldn't have been fair to her.

To have sex with her just because it felt good, just because I've had a crush on her for a super long time, right? I mean, we're different people now.

Why the hell am I even doing the honorable thing? Aren't guys in their twenties supposed to be complete manwhores? And here I am trying to be nice, and she gets pissed.

Last time I rejected us because I was scared, worried, take your pick... oh also, yeah, pissed.

This time, I was just... trying to be a man.

"Yeah, and look how that worked out. She slammed the door in our face." Fuck, I'm literally staring at my dick and talking to it like it's my best friend when all it did was betray us last night the minute we saw her tits in that shirt.

But seriously, those tits.

The cold shower is doing nothing but pissing me off and making my dick feel like it's about to freeze off.

I quickly wash off, grab a towel and check my phone.

She hasn't texted at all. I don't really blame her, but at least say, oh hey, you alive? Or maybe something like, ready for today's challenge?

Ugh, why does it feel like I'm waiting for my date to text

me back? It's not like last night was a date; it was more like me feeling desperate to talk to someone, thinking of her constantly, and, you know, sitting on her couch while watching a creepy documentary about squatters. And they say romance is dead!

I should have one hundred percent gone for a Ryan Gosling movie or Ryan Reynolds. Fuck, why didn't I just stick with the Ryans?

Rookie mistake.

Not that it was a date.

Not that I went there with dark intentions.

I'm driving myself crazy as I quickly get ready. At this point, I'm not even surprised when the doorbell rings, and I go to check only to see another tracksuit in red.

Oh good, ADIDAS is sponsoring this chaos.

Awesome.

I grab the package along with the white shoes and put everything on, then go across the hall and stand in front of her door.

I'm not sure how long I stand there, but the door eventually opens, making whatever the hell I'm doing look way creepier than intended.

Ivy's wearing an identical outfit, and she frowns at me. "How long have you been standing there?"

"Seconds." I lie flippantly. More like minutes where I was trying to figure out what to say without getting kneed in the balls. "You ready?"

She shrugs. The door closes. So far, things aren't starting off well.

We walk in silence to the elevator.

I don't think things can get worse after yesterday, but her silence is damning. I hate it so much. I wish I could just poke her more, annoy her. Damn, I miss my stupid stapler; at least it made her look at me.

"Yo," I choke out. "Did you sleep okay?"

She slowly cranes her neck to stare up at me. "Are you high?"

"No." I wish. "I was just checking since it was so late and all."

"It was like one in the morning, not that late, and we got to sleep in. Are you sure you're ready to perform today?"

Perform. Perform. Perform. I would perform the hell out of her right now if she'd just let me and if I wasn't trying to be a good person. "Yeah," I finally say, voice cracking. "I'm on point."

"Suuuure." She rolls her eyes. "Look, I need this job, so don't mess shit up for me, okay?"

"Someone's prickly this morning," I grumble.

"Someone got left hot and bothered last night, so forgive her for being prickly, you piece of—"

The elevator doors open. Max steps in.

"Perfection." She quickly adds. "Male perfection, the best partner I've ever had, truly, I won the lottery, ha, ha." She elbows me so hard I gasp.

Max looks between us. "Are you both up to the third challenge?"

"Never better," I choke, giving him a thumbs up.

He sniffs the air, then looks between us. "Hmmm, interesting."

What the hell was that?

Ivy and I share a look.

Her eyes are wide.

Mine mirror hers.

Max turns back to look at us. "It's a good partnership, yes, I think it's a good one, might be a bit chaotic, but those are always the best ones."

"Is he talking about us?" I mouth to Ivy.

She pinches my side.

I jerk in response.

Max chuckles his back to us as the elevator doors open again. "Come along little ducklings, or as I like to say, 'lings.'"

"I'm so confused," I say under my breath.

Ivy loops her arm in mine like she needs an anchor as Max's boat just sails off to sea. "Same."

I'm not even mad about it as I hold her close and walk behind him to meet the rest of the teams in the lobby.

Anderson looks ready to punch me in the face when he sees my arm linked with Ivy's, and Jude smirks like he knows our secret, like he knows we kissed.

What is this, middle school?

"Attention." Dustin clears his throat and adjusts his bowtie about a dozen times before clapping his hands. "Today's challenge will be a mash-up of the first and second challenges."

"Does that mean death?" I whisper under my breath, earning another elbow from Ivy.

But seriously, does that mean death?

"Today is a wonderful day!" Max announces. It's now that I realize he's wearing this loud blue pinstriped suit along with shiny shoes and a hat like he's ready to go to the Kentucky Derby.

Oh no, are we about to be horses?

And again, will we die?

"You will race," Max announces. "And first to finish gets ten extra points; as of right now, Ivy and Jack are in first, with

Ruby and Jude in second; those are the ones to beat. Are you ready to hear the next challenge?"

"Yes!" Anderson yells.

"Love the enthusiasm!" Max points. "Dustin, give him an extra point for the yell."

"Yes, sir." Dustin dabbles on his iPad.

How is this even fair?

"Anyway…" Max chuckles. "As you know, we have products for the hotels you've already had to try out. You'll be using those products while also playing Honey, If You Love Me. A classic, *classic* nineties game. I think church youth groups were scandalous enough to even use them, right Dustin?"

Dustin rolls his eyes.

Max grins. "He was the captain of the Bible Squad."

"It was Quiz Team," Dustin mumbles. "And I still beat you."

"Hah!" Max laughs. "Anyway…" He clears his throat. "The goal of the game is to get the person whose lap you're sitting on to smile. And mind you, we're all about a zero sexual harassment policy, so you don't need to sit on the other person's lap; not a requirement; we will have sensitivity gamers for each team to make sure you're comfortable. We don't want any lawsuits, so please use your imaginations; how could you possibly make the person, your enemy, your partner—smile."

I actually smile hearing this.

It wouldn't take much for me to crack with her.

But anyone else?

I'm Stone Cold Steve Austin.

I've got this.

"We've got this," I whisper to Ivy.

She pales. "I'm horrible at this game."

"What?" I pull away. "How?"

"I crack under pressure!"

"Well, that's not helpful!" I hiss. "You have to keep it together, think about something really sad, like dead puppies, death, a kitten who just got abandoned by its mom!"

She shoots me a glare. "What the hell is wrong with you?"

"Sorry." I look away. "I was just trying to make you sad."

"Yeah, thanks! What I always wanted! To cry!"

"The puppy and kitten aren't real; that helps, right?"

She takes a deep breath. "We have to watch out for Jude's eyes. They're too blue."

"Look away." I nod. "And if you start to smile or react, just think about how tiny his dick is."

She jerks her head in my direction. "When have you ever seen his dick?"

I gazed at him in speculation. "We used to work out together to get rid of the rage from the internship stress. His dick is so small I wonder if he cries himself to sleep at night."

"You're lying."

"If bro got a boner, you'd think that his fly was just undone, trust me on this."

She angles a glance at Jude.

I elbow her. "Stop it; that's weird."

"And you staring at his tiny dick isn't?"

"I was confused!" I hiss. "I was like, where is it, where's his dick."

"Why the hell were *you* searching, Jack?"

"Don't make this weird!"

"Too late!"

"...and those are the rules!" Max claps his hands. "Now, you and your partner have ten minutes to plot— Oh, and one final addition. The winning two teams get to have happy hour as a bonus! And if you're sober, you get a very fancy strawberry lemonade. YUM!"

Ivy suddenly grabs me by my shirt. "We have to win!"

"Because of the lemonade?" I laugh.

"The vodka. Because of the vodka, Jack."

I nod. "That's fair; let's kill these bitches."

"Word." She laughs, raises her hand, and I slap it

Suddenly I feel lighter than I did this morning and more resolute.

We have to win.

I have to get the girl whose lips I still taste—her drink.

And I want to be the man sitting across from her watching her drink it.

CHAPTER
Eight

Ivy

It's ride or die at this point.

I know Jack can do this; just by walking around the small circle, he has every girl on the other teams swooning toward him; they'd probably just hold off so he'd sit on their laps.

Perverts. All of them.

I glare while Jack makes his rounds.

And as I watch him, I think about last night, about our steamy kiss. His eyes fall to mine; no, they simply stare straight through me; a small smirk spreads across his face.

I need to look away.

I can't.

His walk is smooth as he moves around the small circle of teams, and then he suddenly jumps right on Jude's lap like a toddler, wraps his arms around him, and leans in like he's going to kiss him. "Honey, honey, oh baby girl…" He starts smooshing Jude's cheeks together, earning chuckles from everyone. "If you love me, if you truly"—he touches his forehead against Jude's, winks—"Truly, love me..." And honest to God, Jack starts to shed a tear. "Love me." People start dying from laughter. "Will you please, please, please, for the love of God..." He jumps off Jude's lap and falls to his knees in front of him. "...smile?"

Jude's lips are quivering.

I'm praying.

I need this happy hour.

And Jack cinches the deal when he does a little spider crawl with his fingertips up Jude's thighs. "Pretty please, boo?"

Jude bursts out laughing, then shoves Jack away. "That's cheating."

"Not cheating that you want me, boo." Jack winks again and then gives me a thumbs up and joins the seat next to me.

I'm still as Jude takes his turn. He prowls around the circle, tries a few girls and guys, then finally looks over at me, then Jack.

Oh shit.

So far nobody has taken the bait.

I don't think I will, but I'm worried now.

He stops in front of me and very slowly goes down to one knee; I immediately start to panic, seeing flashbacks of the proposal that happened but was wrecked last year before taking this internship by my stupid ex-boyfriend, who isn't even worth talking about.

I feel myself shake for entirely different reasons as Jude grabs my hand, the same way that my ex did when he professed all his love and gave me a promise ring out of guilt for cheating on me, which he also drunkenly confessed that same day.

Asshole.

I really liked him. Did I love him yet? No, but it doesn't help that the girl he cheated with is someone I'd once considered a friend or that the same girl used to always say how lucky I was to have him.

All guys should burn.

I jerk my hand away from Jude and give Jack a panicked look like I need him to step in or save me; I don't really know what to do at this point, we've already won one round, and I don't feel like smiling.

Jude eventually gives up and walks to some other random girl that I can't see through the tears of frustration in my eyes. When everyone has a chance to go, Max steps back in with Dustin behind him and gives a new challenge.

"All right, you've all done very well, but now we up the stakes. Everyone will be blindfolded. I know it feels like it defeats the purpose, but you have to not only keep a straight face but try to guess based on the two clues Dustin reads off— who the person in front of you is. Ivy, you'll go first."

This seems semi-hard. Most of the interns work together, but not all of us are close, and right now, I'm a little bit of a hot mess. I get handed a blindfold and put it on while everyone else is handed theirs.

"All right, Dustin will lead you to the person you need to convince to smile; remember, you have to both make them smile and guess accurately to get a point for your team."

"Okay." I stand, and a hand gently touches my lower back and leads me to the side. "Is everyone still sitting in the same place, or did everyone get shuffled."

"Everyone," Max says, with humor lacing his voice, "has been shuffled around, and they no longer have their blindfolds on; you may begin when you're ready!"

Crap, I'm led toward someone.

"Am I allowed to touch them?"

"Only good touch," Max says out loud. "And ask permission; we don't want to get sued, ha, ha."

"Again," Dustin mutters behind me.

"It was the goat's fault, and I'm not changing my story!" Max insists.

It's the distraction I needed because what the heck did the goat do—you know what, never mind, I can't even process the insanity that is our CEO right now. What's his thing with farm animals anyway?

"Okay," Dustin says behind me. "You have two minutes to make them smile."

"Them?"

"We let people decide their own labels here, Ivy. Company policy." Max says in a stern tone that almost makes me roll my eyes. I mean, I'm all for it. I just wish I knew if the person in front of me was Jude so I don't experience more flashbacks of the cheating drama with the ex.

I take a deep breath. "Okay, what are the hints first?"

"Loves coffee. Teases. Oh yes, and he—thank you, good sir—has given permission to let you know that his favorite candy is vanilla Tootsie Rolls—bro, same! Got the five-pounder last night from Amazon, primed that shit so hard, so hard, like you don't even know—"

Dustin clears his throat.

And Max just has to add. "...but like, the cherry's good too. What? I want to be inclusive!"

"Two minutes start now," Dustin says, and I'm standing in front of this guy, wondering who the hell—wait a second...

I think back.

Jack used to only buy that random children's craft candy and give it out like it was the cool kind at Halloween. And in high school he'd constantly pop the Tootsie Rolls in his mouth when he was testing.

But lots of people like Tootsie Rolls, right?

I lean in, not realizing how close I am until I can literally feel him breathing, then put my hands on his shoulders.

I know those shoulders.

I know the weighted breaths he's taking.

I know his smell.

I smile and then turn my head to the side of his. This is Jack, not like my Jack; wait, when did Stapler Boy become My Jack? No, like my partner, yes, that's it. Partner. I know it. I know it's him.

I get right up close to his cheek, then whisper in his ear. "Bet I could get you to smile if I kissed you."

I cup his face with my hands, then whisper again. "I'll take you on a Tootsie Roll date and even let you bring the stapler—wait, would that be a triple date?"

Time's running out, and he isn't budging.

So, I do what any desperate girl does in a weird situation.

I lean forward and press a kiss to his lips, then pull back and say, "Bet I know what would really make you smile." And trail my hand down his chest and say again. "Remember the time Marselle shit her pants after eating all those beans on the class trip and lied to one of the football players that it was chocolate, and he tried to eat it?"

Laughter follows.

Including his.

"Come on, that was seventh grade!" he yells, then tugs down my blindfold and licks his lips. "Bet it was tasty."

Wait, is he talking about shit or me?

His eyes go to my mouth, then back up again, and then he reaches for me. I'm literally in this weird trance with his gorgeous eyes and don't even remember that people are around us.

"We're totally getting sued," Dustin grumbles under his breath.

"Nah, she's right." Jack smiles. "I liked it. Well played."

We high five, and I leave the game.

The rest of the hour only one more team gets taken down, and it's Jude's. He couldn't get the dude to so much as budge; I mean, he got even more desperate than me, going as far as to ask if he could tickle the guy's feet.

Or suck his toe.

I mean to each his own, right?

At the end of the competition, we reign victorious. Anderson and his partner came in second. I can almost taste the margaritas on my tongue when Dustin approaches, still in his stark black-rimmed glasses, what looks like ironed jeans, and a blue button-up that's tucked severely tight into said jeans. "Follow me."

"He's totally going to have a nervous breakdown," Jack whispers under his breath.

I snort out a laugh. "His boss is Max; what do you expect?"

"Never work for family."

"Never," I agree.

Dustin sighs. "I can hear you."

"Sorry." Jack coughs out a laugh. "Thought we were being quiet."

"I lack in many ways." He looks over his shoulder. "But my ears are a gift from God."

"Ummmm." I give him a thumbs up. "Good for you."

He rolls his eyes and opens the door to the outside parking lot, where a black van is waiting. "Get in."

"Wait, are we being kidnapped?" Jack asks, holding up his hand, then grabbing my wrist like he needs to protect me.

Kiss. Kiss. Kiss.

I need to forget about our kiss and about his amazing smell and— Wait! Kidnap? He did say kidnap, right?

Dustin looks heavenward. "You aren't getting kidnapped. This is your ride to your happy hour for the top two teams with the most points. Drink responsibly. Wear a condom. World peace." He aggressively opens the van door. "Well? You getting in or not?"

"Question," Jack asks as we get in the van. "What does world peace have to do with condoms and drinking responsibly?"

Dustin's eyes are haunted as he whispers, "Everything." Then he shuts the door in our faces.

I gulp. "Yeah, something's not right with him."

The driver's door opens, revealing Dustin yet again. "Heard that."

"Sorry." I shoot him a too-sunny smile.

He puts on a pair of aviators and looks at us through the rearview mirror; actually, he glares, it wasn't much of a look, and then he starts the engine.

"Do you feel unsafe? Because I feel unsafe," I mutter under my breath, earning another glare from Dustin before he puts the car in drive.

Jack reaches across and grabs my hand and holds it.

He just holds it.

My enemy and partner in crime right now is holding my hand, and his hand isn't clammy. It doesn't feel weird. It feels right. Which is terrifying because why would it feel so good? Why would everything feel so good with someone who I can't even stand to look at while working?

I try to pull my hand away, but he doesn't let me. After I fight for a few seconds in vain, he grips it harder and then puts it on his thigh, then leans back and closes his eyes.

I don't know why, but I like this side of him.

I like it when he's playful and forceful like he knows me better than I know myself, and I like that he's brave enough to put my hand close enough to his dick, knowing full well I'd punch it if he tried anything.

And they say romance is dead.

I smile, then close my eyes too, relaxing my hand on his thigh and wondering where it all went wrong before it went right.

CHAPTER
Nine

Jack

fter holding her hand, I suddenly feel like I'm back in middle school, going to skate night, and wishing I could ask a girl to skate with me for boys' choice. Like, what the hell is wrong with me?

I feel like I just went through a horrible case of puberty and no longer know what to do with my hands when I'm sitting. Do I cross my arms? Do I rest them on the desk? Do I grab my phone?

I'm uncomfortable, and she's beautiful.

That's really the only assessment I have.

I'm so pumped we won, but now I'm like, "is this a date?" Because it feels like a date. We're downtown at a sick bar that probably charges fifty bucks a napkin, and all I can think about is how pretty she looks sipping her Manhattan.

And what's even worse?

She didn't order a diet soda and vodka, though there's

nothing wrong with that. No, she straight-up ordered a Manhattan with Pendleton.

Is it weird that I got hard just hearing her order?

Fuck, I'm so screwed.

Her pink lips touch the martini glass as she sips. I try to lean back in the booth and exhale, then reach for my drink. Is she still wearing that damn pheromone perfume?

Because she smells amazing.

I'm dizzy from it, but in an intoxicating way that has me holding my drink halfway to my mouth like an idiot while she tilts her head at me like she's wondering if I'm gonna make it through the night.

"So…" She finally breaks the silence, sets her drink on the table, and leans forward. "We're basically going to destroy everyone, right?"

"Right," I agree with a smile. "Mainly because we're so good at Squid Game aka Max's Ministrations."

Her laugh sends a jolt to all the wrong and right places. "Kind of has a ring to it, Max's Ministrations."

"We would be unwise to encourage his madness."

"Cheers to that." She lifts her drink again, tilts it back, and then motions for our waiter.

I immediately hate him. Dave… Who's named Dave these days anyway? Dum-dum Dave smiles dumbly down at her. He has piercings in both ears, sandy blond hair, and a megawatt smile that needs to disappear. "Another drink?"

"Shots." She shoots me a grin. "For me and my… partner here."

"Partner," Dave repeats, then looks at me and back at her. "Ohhhhhh, partner, congrats. I'm all for same-sex marriage. Good for you."

I nod and then realize that means he thinks I'm a girl, right? Wrong? Or wait, what? I don't want to be offensive, but I truly want to just pull out my cock and then pee all around the table, like what the fuck?

"I meant in crime." Ivy laughs. "But that works too."

"No. Doesn't work." I grit my teeth. "She's my girlfriend. Two shots, top shelf, tequila, salt, lime. Go, go, go. I promise we'll tip well."

Dave's shoulders slump. He shoots me a glare, then smiles at Ivy and struts off like he's packing, which, no way, I saw his hands and his feet. If he has a big dick, then I quit.

"That was rude." Ivy rests her elbows on the table and yawns.

I point at his disappearing form. "He basically accused me of being this cockless thing sitting across from you because he was trying to hit on you."

"He so was not trying to hit on me." Ivy laughs. "He was taking our order."

"No. Disagree. Nope. Not it." I hold both hands out and put them behind my head. "He most definitely was trying to hit on you."

Ivy rolls her eyes. "And you're the expert on this how?"

"Manwhore." I point at myself. "Recognizes manwhore."

"Oh, and he finally admits it."

"Please." I nearly growl. "It's not like it's a secret that I was pretty much the worst. You were better off without me."

"Yeah, could have caught something."

"Whoa, whoa, whoa, I said manwhore, not stupid manwhore, I always used protection, and it's not like I just went around throwing my dick everywhere. I made careful choices."

"Careful. Choices," she repeats and then bursts out laughing. "Why couldn't we have had the shots before this conversation?"

As if on cue, Dave brings our shots.

I glare again.

He glares back but walks away.

Probably spit in both of them, but whatever.

I take the shot and hand Ivy hers. "Well, now we have them."

"Cheers." She takes the glass. "To…"

"Partners." I throw in.

She laughs.

How do I get her to do that all the time? And why the hell does that feel like a weird request? What the shit is going on with me lately?

It's like she broke me, and now I just want her to touch me only so she can fix me and make it all better… and fuck, now I'm thinking about her in a nurse's outfit. And great, I've been staring at her for longer than necessary like a total stalker; that seems to be my new thing. Some people develop good habits like working out and eating celery—then some people end up on Dateline.

Sad to say, it's looking bleak for me at this point if I keep just staring at her mouth.

"Partners." She clinks her glass against mine, smile easy, pretty. "Are you sure you're okay? You've been weirder than normal."

I start chugging my Manhattan like a boss and nearly choke on the cherry while trying to simultaneously nod at her. "Yup, yup, yup, so good, everything's great, glad we won."

"Worth it." She nods.

In the back of my head, I wonder if we should just stick with one type of liquor, but I ignore that still small, *wise* voice and keep ordering shots of tequila with my Manhattans until I see three of Ivy and can no longer count how many fingers I possess on either hand.

I mean, I know there should be five on each.

But my eyes keep telling me I have seven.

It makes no sense.

It also makes me laugh a bit.

"Seven," I mutter with a grin and reach for my drink. "Wait, how is this empty?"

Ivy shakes her head. "Because you're on your third one, and you keep ordering shots and just chugging everything in front of you. Do you need fries? Should we order fries? Because I've heard fries help when you're completely wasted and ready to fall off your bar stool."

"I'm not gonna farl off mya bar shtool," I grunt.

She laughs. "You realize you already did, right?"

Panic sets in. "What?"

"Yeah, it was, um…" She leans in and crooks her finger. "Right after you pissed your pants and started yelling about being the King of the World. Tears followed because, you know, Leo's passing and all."

"LEONARDO DI CAPRIO DIED!" I wail. "Son of a bitch!" I jump to my very unsteady feet. Huh, did I untie my shoes? Did they untie themselves? I laugh because, for some reason, it's funny, but then I remember Leo. "Why didn't he just hold on, Ivy? Why?"

Ivy's eyes are wide with amusement. "Why indeed?"

"And he couldn't have just—" Am I crying? No, it's the dust again, all the dust; my eyes do feel blurry. "It's almost like I'm on that very ship." I nod. "Sail away, sail away, sail away…" I can't stop singing Enya; it just bursts past my lips without my permission as I sway in front of the table. I am seriously wasted, and I'm singing to Ivy.

"You know—" I point at the three of her. "When he's frozen there, I legit thought he would make it." I shake my head. "We will not forget your sacrifice! We will not go quietly into the night!" I shout. "Because today is our Independence Day!"

Ivy holds her stomach and laughs so hard that I'm convinced I just nailed happy hour. I mean, she's happy, I'm happy.

Fuck, Leo's still dead, but we did win against the aliens. "USA, USA, USA!"

"Alllllright big guy." Ivy grabs my hand and then wraps an arm around me. "While I do enjoy you quoting random movies and somehow becoming more charming than usual, people are gonna start complaining, so let's go back to the apartments and sleep this off."

"I'll sleep you off," I snap.

"Good threat." She pats me on the chest. "Very good threat."

"It's a promishhh…" I'm suddenly exhausted. "Hey, do you think we can go to Leo's funeral? Or light a candle?"

Ivy leads me out of the restaurant. "Yeah, big guy, let's do that right after we thank Bill Pullman for his epic speech."

"Fucking love Bill Pullman," I say. "He's an American treasure, and nobody can tell me differently. He's like Keanu, KEANUUUUUUU!"

She claps a hand over my mouth as we leave the bar, and I can barely see when we get into a waiting car.

Cool trick.

We just had a black car waiting.

Oh yeah, because we won.

What did we win again?

My head lolls to the side as the lights pass by in a blur; the last thing I remember is looking up at Ivy and saying, "Bet Keanu can't do this."

CHAPTER
Ten

Ivy

I've never seen him so drunk in my entire life. It's like he was just blindly taking tequila like it was water, and then to make matters worse, I had to help him into his apartment, which didn't really work out as planned since he couldn't find his damn key fob.

So here we are.

Him snoring on the couch in *my* apartment.

Me lying in my bed, wishing I could put a pillow over his head just so he stops snoring and a lot of moaning from his end. And not the good moaning, the whole, I'm gonna wake up soon and probably puke all over the carpet moaning.

I finally fall asleep around two in the morning, only to wake up an hour later to the sound of a toilet flushing and more moans.

"Sleeeep!" I yell.

"So sorry, was busy puking out my brains." Comes right back. "Hey, the couch is super uncomfortable. Can I just crash with you?"

"You have an apartment!" I remind him.

"Too much energy." And then my door's getting opened, and Jack's stumbling into my room and throwing himself onto the king-sized bed. "Hold me. I'm sad."

"No!" I almost laugh. "You're not sad; you're just still drunk!"

"Whose idea was the shots?" he grumbles into his pillow. "Demon woman."

I jerk the blankets away from him. "Clearly the drunk person's."

"I hate drunk persons." He turns on his side. "I puked once, brushed my teeth, wait, was that your toothbrush—"

"Are you kidding right now?"

He laughs. "There was a spare in the bathroom, most likely from Dustin stockpiling these apartments and getting worried about being fired."

"I'm sure that's a daily concern where Max is concerned." I take a deep breath and exhale. "Now, I need sleep. Which means if you're going to just lay there breathing heavy, at least make yourself useful and attempt to even out the mattress."

"I'm sorry, what?"

"You know." I toss on my side, "Even out the mattress, where equal parties do their part in making sure that nobody just rolls into the middle."

"The hell kind of mattresses have you been sleeping on?"

Single ones.

Ones without other people.

I stay silent. "Just... stop talking."

"No, I'm genuinely concerned that you think this is a thing."

"How are you so sober?"

"Water?" His answer. "No, but seriously, this whole mattress balance act, how does it even work if we're having sex."

"WE ARE NOT HAVING SEX."

"IN THEORY!" he snaps. "I'm not stripping you naked right now, am I?"

Why does that make me want to say something snappy like, you should, or you wish, or I guess that's not snappy; it's just immature.

"Why are we yelling again?" I whisper.

He lowers his voice. "You started it."

"Very mature." I pound the pillow beneath my cheek and stare at him. Who looks that hot after getting drunk and puking? Life isn't fair.

"Yes, I've been known to be addressed as an adult from time to time." He leans in. I can smell his minty breath, and I hate that I'm tempted to kiss him.

Hello, he just vomited up half of Tijuana from that mouth.

Right?

And he's only kind of sexy.

His eyes lower to my mouth. "Explain this whole mattress thing before I fall asleep between your boobs."

"Huh?" I shake my head. "How would you accidentally fall asleep between my boobs?"

"Did I say accident?"

"Men." I roll my eyes.

He grins. "I remember them being soft, and like I said, I'm sad. I feel like shit and deserve an award."

"I'll buy you a trophy tomorrow," I deadpan.

"Promise?" He laughs, and I join in because I can't not laugh and maybe because I'm a little buzzed too and a lot exhausted.

"At least one for participation," I add, tucking my hands under my head while he scoots closer to me.

"Those shouldn't even be allowed. You either win, or you lose. Teaching the youth of today that you get a high five for trying is like, I don't know, giving a dude a high five for knowing where to stick it but getting no orgasm in the process. Wow, as I'm talking I realize how inappropriate and weird that just sounded, yet I just couldn't stop."

I burst out laughing. "And you're concerned about my mattress? You just went from kids' participation trophy to sticking it to someone and leaving them wanting."

"Hey!" He smacks me lightly on the ass, the duvet padding the light sting. "I never leave anyone wanting."

"Ummmmm... do you not remember the other day?"

"How could I forget?"

We're both quiet.

I clear my throat. "Anyway, we should sleep; big day of torture tomorrow."

"Sleep, sure." He wraps an arm around me and then tugs me close. "But first things first, I have a job to do." I'm spooned up against him.

"Wh-what are you doing?" I ask.

"Making the mattress equal, also known as spooning in the middle, now go to sleep before I'm tempted to show you just how thorough I can be when participating..." He kisses me on the forehead.

I melt a little.

Then I want to kick him for making me want to melt and for confusing me so much. We're just partners in forced proximity, which makes feelings confusing.

Plus, we're both competitive, so really, he just wants to win when it comes to any and every argument.

I stiffen.

"Relax." His breath tickles my ear. "Sleep."

"This means nothing." Even as I say it, I'm snuggling closer to him and throwing my leg over his. We both adjust until we're plastered against one another. He's so warm.

"Agreed," Jack finally answers. "It's just participation."

"Just participation." I yawn against his neck.

His hands start running through my hair.

Funny how participation suddenly feels like winning.

CHAPTER
Eleven

Jack

I don't want to move.

My head's pulsing with a headache from hell, and I'm starving, but she's laying across me, both legs somehow pretzeled between mine, her hair's all over the place, across my chest, next to my mouth, my shoulder, it's like she was attempting to see how much of herself she could get on me throughout the night.

So why am I not moving?

Partnership was either the best idea I've ever had or the worst. My heart's already way too involved, and my brain's screaming that we should have just stayed away.

Because we knew this would happen, like seeing the cliff, dancing alongside it, and convincing yourself that you won't eventually fall off the side, knowing full well that when you do, you'll either crash and burn or land in the ocean and survive.

Jury's still out on that one.

She moves against me, her hands sliding down my side until she grazes the front of my briefs.

I bite down on my lower lip to keep from moaning out loud; her hand flutters by again. I'd almost prefer getting punched in the dick because this is torture. I want to move my hips toward her so bad that it hurts.

She does it one more time. I pump against her fingertips.

Her hand freezes.

I squeeze my eyes shut in frustration.

And then she starts to palm me through my briefs, and I'm so close to exploding all over her and myself that I can't even be embarrassed.

"Participation trophy," she mutters.

"If I had known," I rasp as she continues to press hard on my cock, "that this was the trophy, I wouldn't have slept last night."

Her hand inches along the band of my briefs, and I hold my breath until she reaches inside and grips me.

"Shit, shit, shit," I nearly come off the bed. "I'm so sensitive."

She strokes up and down. "At least you weren't lying about being big."

"Never lie about dick size," I say through clenched teeth. "They'll always find out anyway." I open my eyes and stare down at her. She's not looking at my dick; she's looking at me. "Your hand feels like torture."

"Imagine what my mouth would feel like," she teases, her eyes sleepy.

"Fuck!" I fall apart all over her hand as if I'm twelve.

And all it took was her staring at me, stroking me, then mentioning her mouth.

I'm a panting, sticky mess.

She releases me and smiles up at me. "Thanks for keeping the mattress equal."

"Any day, night, afternoon, brunch, I'm your guy," I whisper, wanting to kiss her so badly.

Instead, I pull off my shirt, wipe off her hand, and clean up. She doesn't seem to mind at all, though, and lays back down next to me, so I toss my shirt to the bedroom floor and do the same.

Soon she's lying on my chest, and I'm pretending that this is normal, that we have a cease-fire after all the hell we've been through.

I pretend she's more than a partner, but mine.

Soon both of us fall asleep.

Only to wake up to the sound of the doorbell.

"The hell?" I jolt awake, then look at my phone. "Oh shit! Up, up, up! We have to get up!"

Ivy startles awake, then slaps me across the face.

"What the hell, Ivy!"

"You scared me! I thought you were an intruder, and I had a dream about—" She looks over at my discarded shirt, then back at me. "Never mind."

"Not a dream; that was reality," I point out. "Now get your ass out of bed. We're going to be late!"

"You're welcome for the hand job!" She sticks out her tongue.

"Trust me, I could have died happy, but we have to compete, remember?"

Her eyes narrow as she jumps out of bed, and my eyes can't decide if we should stare at her ass or just squeeze shut, so we aren't tempted.

"Back to enemies?" She crosses her arms, and her breasts could not look more perky if they tried. "Hey, eyes up here!"

"Sorry!" I shake my head. "It's just they're right there, and I have eyes!"

She looks down at my dick. "Sorry, it's just right there, and I have eyes."

"Touché," I grumble and do a slow turn. "Look, I'll get the door, you find some protein bars or something, and we'll meet in the kitchen."

"Fine." She rolls her eyes.

"Fine." I mimic her voice and then nearly trip over my own feet as I run into the living room and pull open the door.

Dustin stands there in a blue shirt, polka dot tie, and jeans. "You're going to be late."

"I know; we're hurrying." I run my hands through my hair as he looks past me and then back at me. "Isn't this Ivy's apartment?"

"Yep, be down in a few; thanks bye!" I shove the door in his face, panicking a bit as Ivy runs down the hall in black joggers and a matching sweatshirt. She grabs her slides by the door and then goes into the kitchen.

"Protein bars, protein bars, protein bars." She looks around the pantry, grabs something, opens the fridge, tosses me a cold brew, and then grabs her sunglasses and purse. "What?"

I realize I'm just standing there like a shirtless idiot, but damn, I've never seen a girl get ready so fast. "That was fast."

"I can be fast." She smiles.

I know we're in a hurry, but I can't help it. I stroll over to her, pull her against me and kiss her on the mouth, it's hard, brief, and random as hell, but I can't help myself anymore.

"Wh-what was that for?" Her lips are even flushed.

"Just think of it as a participation trophy, you know, from

this morning." I wink, earning a shove from her. "Let me run across the hall and grab a shirt, then we can go."

"Could have used the same shirt from last night, but…" She looks away, cheeks pink.

"But then I'd have to explain why I have dried—"

"Ew, gross, just go."

"Wasn't 'ew, gross' this morning," I grumble as she shoves me out of the apartment and into the hall.

"Not the time to discuss; just grab a shirt; I'll wait here." She shoves the food into her purse along with her unopened cold brew. I'll never fully understand why every girl I know seems to take after Mary Poppins when it comes to their bags.

She probably has a first aid kit in there too.

Hell. after these last few days, we might need one.

I open my door and run down the hall to the master, grabbing the first clean shirt I can, an old vintage band shirt that's really soft and won't look dumb with my gray sweats. I grab my ADIDAS slides and hurry back out into the hall.

Ivy's staring at her phone in horror.

"What? What's wrong?" I immediately think it's bad news.

She glances at me, then back at the screen, and finally, she looks back up at me. "Please tell me you liked Nickelodeon when you were a kid."

"Who didn't?"

"Oh, thank God." She turns the phone to me. "Because according to this text from Anderson, who's already downstairs waiting with everyone else… Max just mentioned nostalgia and already handed out team shirts."

"Oh great, do I even want to know?"

She scrunches up her nose. "It appears we're going to be the Silver Snakes."

"Why does that sound familiar?"

"Because…" She sighs. "It's from Legends of the Hidden Temple."

I freeze. "Ivy, wait—"

"Come on, we have to hurry."

"I think I'm going to be sick." Nausea comes over me in waves.

"You already puked up everything last night. Let's go!" She starts to tug at me, but all I can see is his face.

The nightmares.

The T-shirts.

"No, Ivy, like for real, I'm freaking out here."

"It was just tequila!" she says.

"It's not the tequila." I'm ready to hold onto the elevator to keep from having her shove me farther. "It's Olmec."

"Olmec?"

"The rock temple guy—he's terrifying, and his little minions, I may have um, when I was very small, very, very, very—*very* small, wet the bed after falling asleep to reruns on Nick at Night, my mom said I woke up screaming, 'Olmec, Olmec!'"

Ivy's eyes widen. "Jack, I need you! We're a team, and who the hell is scared of Olmec!"

"His voice is loud, and he captures people in his temple, Ivy! I don't know what's more terrifying!"

"Okay, okay" She calmly grabs my hand and pulls me into the elevator. "It's going to be fine. We'll figure it out, but we can't lose, so you need to get your shit together."

"Easy for you to say."

Her eyes narrow. "More participation trophies for your future wall if you can; at the very least, just attempt not to shit your pants if it really is Legends of the Hidden Temple."

"How many more?"

She glares.

"Fine." I cross my arms. "But if Olmec is there, just be warned, you may hear a high-pitched scream from my general direction."

CHAPTER
Twelve

Ivy

I don't exactly know how to calm down a twenty-two-year-old man while he has a nervous breakdown in front of a fake temple.

College did not prepare me for this.

We're wearing our Silver Snake shirts.

He's pale as a ghost.

And we are one hundred percent about to play Legends of the Hidden Temple. Who knew that out of all things in Jack's life, this would be his kryptonite? It's like Ninja Warrior course meets OG Nickelodeon as we have to cross the water by jumping onto a line of floating rafts, run through the temple to grab the hidden treasure, and oh yeah, avoid everyone trying to "kill" us in said temple on top of beating the other teams in every relay race known alive.

But that's not even the worst part.

The worst part.

Olmec.

He hasn't spoken yet, but every few minutes, I see Jack side eye this giant talking rock, and I'm a bit concerned that this is going to be our downfall, the reason neither of us gets our promotion or bonuses.

A rock.

A stupid rock.

"Focus." I elbow him in the ribs. "It's not real."

"Feels real, feels very real," Jack says under his breath.

"You were a kid!" I hiss. "You're a man, be a man, feel your dick, be awesome!"

"Feeling my dick sounds really bad in front of a kids' show I used to watch with a rock scaring me… yeah, that feels wrong on so many levels. New plan, we run."

"No." I grab his hand. "New plan, we listen to Dustin, learn what we're competing in, and win so we can go back to the apartment and have… trophies."

Jack's head pops up. "Real trophies or trophy trophies?"

I roll my eyes. "What's gonna motivate you more? An actual trophy or sex?"

"I GET SEX?" he yells, earning almost every judgmental look imaginable from the other interns, and you know what? Who cares! I want to win, and I like him, and this is so not the time to read into things.

"Yes. Sex. All the sex. I'll sex you so hard," I mutter under my breath. "So, ignore Olmec and focus on me." I take a deep breath. "Repeat after me, be the snake."

"I would snake you so hard—"

"Not the time!" I elbow him again. "Just, remember, you're the snake. Snakes are vicious, cunning, and creepy. We're going to annihilate every single one of them, and then we'll celebrate."

"Fucking Orange Iguanas. Who even comes up with that as a competitive name?" he says.

I snort. "Right, or the Purple Parrots, go cry little birdies into your nest!"

Jack hangs his head. "This has gone downhill so very fast. And all we wanted was a 401K."

I burst out laughing. "Or to be able to afford rent, but yeah, and now we're competing against them. Have we talked about the Blue Barracudas? Because I distinctly remember them always winning."

Jack sighs. "Of course, that's Anderson's team."

"Of course," I agree.

We've been standing in this weird course for the last ten minutes while people run around. There are cameras, which, of course, means we're getting televised to either Max or the world. Who knows at this point anymore? There's a huge film crew as well as people moving objects around that I'm pretty sure I'm going to be jumping over or falling into.

It's like the Indiana Jones ride at Disney, only worse because you don't get to sit in a nice little seat and get shoved through the thing—you've got to experience it.

I reach for Jack's hand and grab on.

The rest of the teams left, Anderson and Jude being the ones behind us with the other two girls whose names I keep forgetting because, well, I'm focused on Jack and me, the Silver Snake Squad.

I take a deep breath as the lights around us lower then flicker back on again, and like a bad dream, or you know, Satan, Max appears in front of us with Dustin.

"Welcome, welcome!" He claps his hands. He's wearing an all-black suit and looking as debonair as ever with his brown hair slicked back. How does his wife even do this? I truly want to know. "I hope you're all surprised with our temple!" He spreads his arms wide. "This will be the second to the last challenge you'll face; the next one will be mental; this one will be obviously more physical as you propel your tiny little bodies through the challenge course and attempt to grab your medallions without getting caught by the soldiers or Olmec!"

Jack flinches next to me.

I squeeze his hand tighter.

"Every one of you will be given a fair chance for your medallions; once you pass your challenges, you'll enter the temple and search each room until you can complete all three pieces. Nostalgia's huge right now, so we will be including The Moat, Steps of Knowledge, Temple Games, and finally the Temple Run."

"Shit," Jack says under his breath. "That's the worst one. They fucking chase you!"

"Shh!" I elbow him in the ribs.

"Is that your thing now? Just bruising my ribs?" He gives me major side-eye, and I momentarily forget he's about ready to pass out from fear. He's so pretty, his perfect mouth that I've tasted way too many times, and his effortless hair, it's like the model hair flip that everyone wishes they could do but can't really execute. Swear sometimes he's in slow motion.

I give my head a shake to get all the thoughts out. "Yes, that's my thing. Until we win this, that's my thing."

"Noted," he whispers.

I stand closer as Max continues to talk about all the wonderful horrors we're about to experience. Everyone's wearing their shirts, and we are given the choice to grab some black spandex leggings to make it easier in the water.

Jack sighs. "That's definitely going to show my junk."

"Been there, seen that." I go to elbow him again, only to have him spin me around and pull me against him.

My breath hitches.

"No more elbowing the same spot. Pick a different one." He winks. "And if Olmec kills me, know it was worth it to hold you like this."

I want to punch him.

How dare he be sweet?

Again.

And make me fall.

Again.

I lift my chin. "He's a rock. You'll survive."

"If you say so." He kisses my forehead, and I know everyone sees despite them all grabbing spandex. I know Max sees, Dustin too.

And I don't really care because his kiss felt warm, and it felt right.

How did this even happen?

He looks down at me, then clears his throat and pulls away. "We should probably get ready, yeah?"

"Sure, yeah," I agree, rubbing my arms up and down as if I'm in a blizzard and need to get warm again. I do a small circle, then feel a tap on my shoulder. Jack hands me the spandex. Wait, was he holding them this entire time? "Oh, whoops!"

"Distracted?" he asks with that sexy smile of his.

I snatch the spandex out of his hands. "Just nervous my partner's gonna shit his pants."

He glowers. "Wait until you see Olmec. Then you'll know."

I roll my eyes. "Yes, because rocks that talk and aren't real terrify me to the point of a nervous breakdown in my twenties."

His eyes widen. "Take it back!"

I lean forward and flick him on the chest. "Never. Now, go change."

Everyone's gone into the bathrooms close by and are already almost all changed. Jack shakes his head, then wags his finger at me. "You'll rue the day!"

"Yeah, sure, okay," I examine my nails. "See you in a few, coward."

Max walks up beside me and watches Jack walk into the bathrooms and slam the door. "He reminds me of myself."

I almost choke on my spit. "Ohh? Why's that?"

"I, too, used to be scared of rocks."

"Come again?" I look over at him.

"They're heavy," is all he says before walking away with a whistle. Is the guy on drugs? I mean, what?

Max suddenly stops and looks over his shoulder. "Oh and, Ivy, remember, fear is what makes us stronger. You're going to have to push him through this, but he'll come out better than ever, and isn't that what partnership is all about? Life lessons? Teachable moments? Chaos? Terror?"

I narrow my eyes at him. "What are you playing at?"

Max just smiles. "Life. That's what makes things interesting. Simply life. Glad you've gotten the chance to participate in our games today. Stay strong; sometimes, the hardest ones to catch are the ones we need the most."

"Huh?"

"Work hard," he adds after a heavy pause.

I have no time to think about it as I run to the bathroom and change into my super tight spandex. My shirt, correction, my Silver Snake shirt, stares back at me, and I weirdly smile because who knew this would be my future?

I did always love this show, which makes me laugh since Jack had nightmares and I had dreams.

Maybe that's what Max was saying.

Sometimes life is just life. One person's dream can be another person's nightmare, can be another person's worst-case scenario. Where I just want to propel myself into the temple, I've got a partner that equates that to jumping out of a plane without a parachute.

I smile at myself in the mirror.

Life. Am I right? Life.

By the time I make it back, all the teams are ready to compete across the moat. They have ropes across each floatation device; they all look like rocks; the flotation devices round and brown, and now I'm worried Jack's going to be triggered. Already he's looking around us for Olmec as if the stone god's just going to appear out of nowhere.

"Focus!" I snap.

He nods his head way too many times, then runs his hands through his golden-brown hair and takes a deep breath. "We've got this. Just don't fall into the water. We get a break after each stage. Do you want to go first or me?"

I think about it for a minute. "Why don't you go first in case Olmec shows up randomly and starts talking?"

His eyes widen. "Do you think that could happen?"

"Bad idea, shouldn't have said that out loud," I grumble, then turn to him and grab him by the shoulders. "Make it across the weird rock rafts with the ropes dangling, and I'll make out with you."

He frowns. "For how long?"

"Ready!" Dustin shouts. "In ten, nine, eight—"

"Long enough!" I smack him lightly on the cheek. "Now, find your A-game and destroy Anderson and Jude's teams, okay? They so don't deserve bonuses, corner offices, or Nespresso machines instead of whatever the hell they feed us now!"

"Nespresso." He nods. "Making out." Another nod. "I like this motivation."

"Atta boy." I slap him on the ass. "And if you hear Olmec, just think about the fact that you can finally conquer your fears!"

He gives me a pitiful look. I almost laugh.

"Three," Dustin continues, "two, one."

The siren goes off, and Jack just jumps onto the first raft without even grabbing the rope above him. The rest of the teams are strategizing differently, trying to go faster by having one jump to one raft followed by the other, but if you fall, you have to start over; both of you do, so I think our strategy is better.

"Come on, Jack!" I yell. "You've got this!"

He's on the third raft. Halfway.

He gets to the fourth just as Anderson falls off the third into the water. Both he and his partner swim back and start over. Jude and his partner look like they're ready to beat us, though.

I just keep yelling.

The pressure's on me now.

Jack jumps onto the other platform and starts yelling for me to go, but the rafts are still moving around from him being on them; I have no choice but to grab the rope first and try to move around using whatever upper strength I have.

"Badass!" Jack yells. "Just like that! Grab the next rope!"

We're still in first place as I swing to the next rope and lightly touch the raft, only to jump to the next one. My arms are burning as I reach the fifth rope. I slip and fall onto the raft, but it's moving back and forth so hard that I'm getting drenched in water, and I can feel Anderson's team, stupid Blue Barracudas, right on my ass.

"Focus!" Jack yells. "Right on me. Focus!"

I nod and get on all fours, then slowly get up and grab the rope. My hands feel like they won't ever be the same as I reach for the next rope and step onto the final raft.

Jack can't help me or reach for me, so it's up to me to jump onto the platform. I almost close my eyes as I propel my body forward and land on the platform next to Jack's bare feet. "Please tell me we won."

He leans down and grabs my hands, pulling me to my feet. "We won!"

"Oh, thank God. My hands are curled like I'm eighty; they burrrrn!"

He starts massaging them and doesn't let them go for the next few minutes as the rest of the teams make it across.

"Better?" he asks, still holding my hands in his.

I look into his eyes, and I lie. "No, they still hurt."

"Then, I guess I'll keep holding them," he whispers. "Good job, Ivy."

"You too, Jack."

Things are perfect; I'm so happy I almost don't register the fear on Jack's face as a stone figure's shoved toward us with flashing lights and fire.

Olmec's voice sounds from the loudspeakers, except it's Max's; we'd have to be idiots not to notice that.

I squeeze Jack's hand as we face our next challenge.

"Teams!" Max, aka Olmec, yells. "Approach my temple!"

"Don't shit your pants," I whisper yell.

Jack's eyes are wide with fear. "No promises."

"Seriously?"

"Yeah, seriously," he adds. "He has free space in my nightmares, so I'm sorry I'm having a nervous breakdown right now!"

"I'll give you a BJ!" I shout.

Anderson and Jude both stutter step and look over at us with their partners. I just shrug because…

Winning.

"What?" Jack does a double take. "Did you just say?"

We're still walking toward Jack's doom. "I'll give you a BJ; just keep it cool."

He suddenly straightens toward me. Wow, is that all it took?

He takes a deep breath. "I want two."

"Son of a bitch, Jack!"

"Two BJ's."

"Jack!"

"ITS A REAL FEAR!"

"One BJ, and I'll let you grab my boobs for ten minutes."

Anderson's jaw drops.

Jude looks ready to switch teams.

Whatever.

"Never offered me that," Jude says under his breath to his partner.

"One BJ," Jack says, taking another step. "Ten minutes of tit time, and I want to go down on you."

I stumble.

Jude's partner hits him.

Anderson curses.

And I laugh. "Is that a reward?"

Jack turns to me and winks. "Yeah, it really is."

What can a girl say?

I do want to be a good partner. "Deal."

"Damn," Jack whispers. "I do love participation trophies."

Same.

CHAPTER
Thirteen

Max

"It's not technically illegal," Max says. Most of the board members seem pissed that Ivy's trying to lure her partner through sex. "They did have a fling once, and clearly, they like each other. I say whatever goes at this point!"

One of the men slams more money onto the table. "She's weaponizing him!"

"She's incredible," another says, voice full of awe. "Besides, didn't she spend the night with him last night?"

Max sighs. "According to Dustin, they were late because they were together this morning, but any sort of details were left out because we're still working on details, aren't we Dustin?"

Dustin makes a noise in the back of his throat and shuffles his feet, then looks away.

"Did you just growl at me, you heathen?" Max asks.

Dustin shakes his head. "Sorry, I think I'm catching a

cold." He clears his throat six more times before making the same noise once more and then examining his fingernails.

"Never hire family," Max says under his breath. "And again, we have no details. Simply pay attention to the game and place your bets on the game board, ladies and gentleman."

Everyone stares at the screen and then down at the game board on the conference table.

Markers are picked.

Bets are placed.

And everything is right in Max's world as he stares out at the incredible game he has prepared for the littles.

"A lot's riding on this for the remaining teams," Dustin pipes up again. "You sure you want to make it more difficult on them just because you think you're some sort of wizardly matchmaker? I mean, it was pure luck last time with the interns. I doubt it's going to happen again."

Max taps his fingers against his chin in deep thought. "But if it could, wouldn't that be worth it? Besides, this time it's not the girl that's terrified; it's the guy that's been acting tough this entire time and just wants to win. Let's see if we can't add more red to Olmec's eyes. He does shoot fire, correct?"

Dustin pauses. "You want him to shoot fire? At people?"

"No, no, no," Max says with laughter. "That would be crazy." Everyone pauses around the table. "I just meant, as a scare tactic, you know? Like… spiders."

"Spiders?" Dustin frowns. "Are we adding spiders now?"

"Do we have spiders?" Max asks.

Dustin sighs heavily. "I believe there's a spider shortage."

"That's a thing?"

"It is now."

"Damn."

Dustin moves around the table. "Why don't we just do the whole fire thing as a scare tactic and call it a day?"

"Spoilsport," Max grumbles, then pounds his fist onto the table. "I've got it!"

"Oh good, the evil genius showed up today," Dustin mumbles.

Swear on all that's holy, Max turns to Dustin and goes, "I'm always an evil genius."

"Pray for America," someone mumbles.

"Heard that." Max grabs the remote to Olmec and grins. "This is going to be the best day of our lives."

Dustin just shakes his head and sighs. "And if they don't perform the way you want them to?"

"Still a game," Max answers, "Still fun for the board of directors, and in the end, someone still wins, so why worry?"

"Oh, you know." Dustin crosses his arms. "Lawsuits. Prison. Those things."

Max waits a minute, then whispers, "I own the law."

Everyone looks around the table as Dustin whispers, "Well, that's comforting."

"LET THE GAMES BEGIN!" Max shouts as he's given access to a giant red buzzer that nobody with an IQ like Max should be given access to.

Board members would always remember how Dustin, under his breath, cursed.

"Shit."

CHAPTER
Fourteen

Jack

So, despite the promise of being able to sink my mouth between my partner's thighs once we're done in the temple of doom and death—I still want to shit my pants as we approach Olmec.

I can't decide if it's my childhood fear.

Or the fact that it's Max's voice coming out of said childhood fear. All I know is that I'm squeezing Ivy's hand so hard I wouldn't be surprised if you couldn't find my DNA on every inch of her skin.

Olmec's eyes are red like fire.

And then, as if the stupid rock god thing can read my mind, actual fire shoots out of his eyes. I stumble back and try not to fall into the water. That has to be a lost point, right? If I fall into the water I just escaped from.

"You've got this." Ivy grips my arm harder. "Just focus."

"Focus?" I repeat. "Focus?" I can't stop saying focus. "On what? His devil eyes or the fires of hell? I mean, seriously? Help me out here!"

"Look at his tiny hands!" she shouts.

A loud noise erupts like a volcano from Olmec's head. "Tiny hands?"

"Think he heard me?" Ivy whispers.

I just shake my head and then lower it. "This is how we die, and yes, Ivy. Yes, I think he fucking heard you."

"I was quiet!"

"TINY HANDS!" Olmec shouts again. This time it's Ivy jumping closer to me, holding on to me, and it's me being a bit arrogant as the rest of the two remaining groups look over at us like they don't know what to do. Meanwhile, I'm holding a promised BJ, sooooo I can't be mad but also still gonna shit my pants.

It's really the weirdest day.

A conundrum, if you will.

Anderson starts grabbing at his partner. Meanwhile, she's backing up and trying to get away from the scary statue. I want to yell same girl, same, but I'm too distracted by the perfect person on my left.

Max, or rather, Olmec-Max shouts again; more fire comes, lava follows, and yet again, my brain reminds me that this means death. The lava has to be fake, but it has the correct approach, as Anderson's partner grabs onto him and then falls backward into the water.

They both splash into it.

A gong sounds, and they're suddenly escorted out by the temple guards in full garb. Grass skirts, scary face paint, pointy objects. "Is there no end to this nightmare?"

"Focus!" Ivy hisses.

"Did I say that out loud?"

"You're shaking." She grits her teeth and grabs me by the chin. "Look at me. Not at Olmec, but me. You've got this. We've got this; we have three teams left—" Another splash sounds. "Two teams, I mean two teams, and we can—" Another splash happens. "What the hell is happening, oh—" She grips my chin harder. "Do. Not. Look."

"That's what people say when you have a spider on you, and they're trying to grab it!" I yell. "That's the worst thing to say to someone, and I don't even mind spiders. What the hell do you mean don't look!"

"Close your eyes!"

"…Remaining teams, you will now go through the Temple of Knowledge!" Olmec's voice booms over the loudspeaker as I start to sweat and squeeze my eyes shut. "You'll need to trust your partner implicitly in this challenge as they will be guiding you up each step. You will both be blindfolded."

"Oh, thank God," Ivy whispers.

"Why? Why are we thanking God? Why are my eyes closed?" Look, I want to be a man; I don't want to be frantic, but what the ever-loving hell am I doing right now?

She elbows me.

I should expect this.

I will have forever bruising.

I hang my head as a blindfold's put around me, and then Ivy and I are tied to each other by our wrists.

Is it horrible that, while being completely terrified, I'm still like, cool, kinky, can we take them home?

Son of a bitch, I need help.

Focus!

"And now!" Olmec announces. "Each remaining team will be given two Questions of Knowledge in order to grab your medallions from the temple. Answer correctly, and you can move up the steps, answer wrong, and you'll be taken to the pit of doom."

I gulp. "Do we want to know what the—"

"Nope," Ivy interrupts. "Just focus. You did good in history class, right?"

History. History. History. Ivy always had her hair pulled back in high school. It was a bit lighter then, and I remember wondering what it would be like to pull it tight and kiss down her neck and—

"Jack?"

"So good at history," I answer. "Like a pro. Aced it." Really, just aced studying her, but how hard can it be, right?

I gulp and wait.

"Silver Snakes!" Olmec-Max announces. "Your first question!"

Fucking Blue Barracudas. I'm already mad, and they haven't even been asked anything yet.

We're destroying them. We have to. I have a BJ on the line. I mean, also a job promotion, money; wait, why is that coming second?

Hah, coming second.

Fuck, my focus is shit!

Focus!

I nod my head way too much and hold Ivy's hand. "Were, um, you good at history? Just asking in case my brain explodes from visions of my CEO as Olmec."

"Flunked."

"Shit, serious?"

She laughs. "I like it when you're afraid."

Despite the total fear, I smile and whisper, "I like it when you're brave."

Her steps falter. I hold onto her and slowly walk up to whatever doom we're about to face and wait.

"What are," Olmec-Max starts, "the seven wonders of the ancient world?"

Panic sets in.

"Both partners," he says. "Get a chance to answer. If you have one wrong answer you'll be sent back down the stairs toward the pit of doom where, sadly, the rest of your teammates, except one, have all fallen into."

"Is there beer there?" I laugh.

Ivy elbows again in that same rib. "Not the time."

"Sorry, I make bad jokes when I'm nervous."

"They actually don't serve beer in Hell," Olmec says like he has legit pit of doom knowledge. "They do have filtered water though, you know, because of the heat and dehydration's a bitch. Anyway!" He cackles, which is almost scarier than him serving water in hell. "You have sixty seconds until the next team takes over. Good luck. May the odds ever be in your favor!"

"We go from Squid Games to Hunger Games?" Ivy mutters. "What is this?"

"Corporate America," I say bitterly. "Corporate America."

"In three, two, one!" Olmec announces.

"Um, there's, um, there's the Hanging Gardens of Babylon!" I shout and hear a ding. "The Great Pyramid of Giza?"

And literally, that's all I can remember.

"Um..." Ivy clings to me hard. "Okay, let me think."

"Forty-five seconds left," Olmec announces.

I sigh. "We can do this. Just think…"

I think back to history class and panic.

"Breathe," Ivy says. "Focus, I think the Colosseum is one of them too?"

Another ding sounds.

We have four left and are running out of time.

I take a deep breath again.

I know we can do this; it's just the pressure.

"Do you really want to go into the pit of doom?" she asks under her breath. "There are temple soldiers there and little tiny Olmecs just ready to devour you whole!"

"Colossus of Rhodes!" I shout. "The Lighthouse, the um, Lighthouse of Alexandria!" More dings. "The temple! Temple of Art—er, Artemis! The Statue of Zeus at Olympia, and… and…"

Ten seconds are left. I can hear the countdown from everyone around me, but I've got nothing, absolutely nothing; all I keep thinking is a stupid Roman road because, yay engineering, you guys killed it.

Agh!

"Mausoleum!" Ivy shouts. "The Mausoleum at Halicarnassus!"

Stunned, my mouth drops open. "Are you serious? How did you know that?"

"Oh." She sounds out of breath. "I was a history minor."

"THE HELL!" I roar. "I almost died!"

"I saved you!" she yells back. "Plus, wasn't it invigorating? Don't you feel more alive? Less dead? Less afraid of Olmec!"

A loud rumble occurs around the set. "You may proceed five steps!"

Olmec still sounds creepy, but I'm so freaked out about the stupid pit of doom I'm happy to walk right toward him.

"That was manipulative," I say.

"And we still won." She laughs.

"If you elbow me again, I swear—"

This time I feel a kiss on my cheek. "Sorry, missed your mouth; maybe next time."

I grunt. "You missed more than my mouth."

"Inappropriate."

"And yet you still owe me."

"And you"—she rubs up against me—"owe me... right?"

I groan out loud. "I would so much prefer burying my face between your—"

"Silver Snakes!"

"Sir, yes sir!" I shout.

Ivy bursts out laughing.

"It appears your competition"—fucking Anderson—"have also made it up five steps. In order for each of you to make it to the Temple Run, you have to answer one more question. If the great Olmec deems it honest and wise, you may proceed and gather your three medallions in the final stage. But remember, this isn't just physical. We promised this would be your second to last test, but for fun"—Oh yeah, sure, fun—"we're combining both mental and physical. Are you ready for your questions?"

No. Shit. "Yes," I say.

Ivy copies it, and stupid Anderson says the same along with Stacey and Britney—God, I hate Britney.

I swear I'm sweating harder.

"Jack." Olmec saying my name causes actual chills. I stand as close to Ivy as possible. "You have two choices. You may either earn this internship and walk right through the temple and gather your tokens, or..." He pauses dramatically. "You can do it as a team, knowing you'll potentially lose everything, but lose together. What's your choice?"

Ivy's breath hitches.

I slowly start to pull away from her.

She stiffens.

"And what happens to my partner?" I ask.

"Well, if they let you go," Olmec says, "then they can still have a chance on their own during the temple run to win, but it will be without you. So, what will you choose? And Anderson same goes for you and Stacey. What is your choice?"

I hear a commotion and then the sound of thunder.

"It seems both Anderson and Stacey have chosen to go on their own. Anderson, you'll be escorted to corporate, Stacey, you'll have to battle the temple guards on your own, but you'll earn an extra ten thousand dollars for each medallion you gather."

Whoops of excitement come up from the contestants who have already lost, and that's when I feel it.

The temple guards.

Is that what Ivy was warning me about?

They're all around us. I can feel their breaths.

Oh, God.

I want so badly to run through that temple straight to corporate. Maybe the me from a few days ago would have.

I sigh deeply and mumble. "I hate you."

"What was that?" Olmec says.

"I'll go through," I say, "with my partner. We're ride or die like that."

Ivy softens next to me. "But you're scared."

"But I have you," I say right back. "And if I die, you're kind of like attached to me, so we'll go down together, a lot more cheerful that way."

I think she's going to elbow me, but instead, she leans her head on my shoulder and then straightens. "Let's win this bitch."

"Bitch is already won." I laugh.

The ground rumbles again beneath us, and the sound of things falling fills the air as our blindfolds are pulled from our faces.

"Oh, good God." I try not to curse as a temple guard glares at me.

"Focus!" Ivy yells amidst the falling rocks around the temple. "Plus, it's not like they're real rocks."

"You'll be given helmets as the rocks are, in fact, real," Olmec just has to add as Temple Guards put hard hats on us.

"Corporate America, and its live burial." I look at the tall pyramid-like rock temple. "Sounds about right."

"You should have brought your stapler," Ivy jokes next to me.

I burst out laughing despite my total fear. "You're right; gonna need that more than beer in hell."

"Imagine how much you can annoy the underworld?"

"Spitting out straight up facts." I laugh. "All right, let's grab our medallions and try not to let the temple guards find us."

We move to the very front. I'm bracing for impact when we reach the top of the stairs and nearly stumble over when I see the temple guards lined up and all three medallions for the Silver Snakes lined up for us.

"Is it a trick?" I ask.

"It's trust," Olmec says. "In any work situation, you need to work with others in order to be able to succeed. Sadly, Stacey will now be working with an intern who volunteers and not her partner who abandoned her for riches and glory."

I snicker a bit because I kind of want to punch Anderson in the dick anyway.

"So," Olmec says again as fire lights a small tunnel toward our medallions and those of the Blue Barracudas. "You now have your final question."

I pause.

Ivy freezes.

"How much?" Olmec asks.

"How much? That's the question?" I repeat. "How much what? What is this?"

"A million!" Stacey answers. Of course, Jude's the one who offered to partner up last minute since Anderson skipped town and temple.

"How much?" Olmec says again.

I look over to Ivy; her eyes search mine, and then she smiles up at me, then creepy Olmec, and she says, "No price."

Jude and Stacey's mouths drop as they look over at us.

"Shall we?" I hold my hand out.

"We shall." Ivy grins, and we take our first step into the temple, trusting each other the entire way, and all I can keep thinking is.

Priceless.

CHAPTER
Fifteen

Ivy

He's not ready to enter the actual temple; I know this, he knows this, the world knows this, and yet we keep walking up the stairs to the final challenge, going through the actual temple where I'm pretty sure Jack will end up in a corner rocking back and forth.

I'm still reeling from his answer.

I grip his hand.

It's sweaty.

I don't mind, though. I don't because I know that it's going to be worth it in the end if we can just get the internship.

My heart beats, but what about after?

What?

I have no answer for that, and I feel dumb because I want to ask him. He's literally shaking next to me.

"Hold it together," I say under my breath. "They're just actors, temple guard actors."

"Easy for you to say." He whimpers. "Does this make me less sexy? Wait, I still get sex, right?"

"Win and you get all the sex," I remind him. "Lose and I'm locking you in a closet with Olmec."

"Whoa, whoa!" Jack stumbles. "Max-Olmec or *Olmec* Olmec?"

I laugh. "Which is worse?"

"Max Olmec. He breathes fucking fire, Ivy!"

"Fair." I laugh as we ascend the final steps of Olmec's temple to gather our medallions.

Jude and Stacey are still halfway up. We won the extra points, so we get the advantage, which is perfect since I know we'll need it like crazy.

Olmec's voice booms. "Let the countdown begin, in ten, nine, eight—"

"Shit, shit, shit." Jack does a little jump next to me, still holding my hand. "Shit."

"You said that already." I smack him and release his hand.

Olmec Max breathes fire out of his mouth. "All you have to do is find three of the medallions that make one of the seven wonders of the ancient world, put them together, and bring them to the top of the pyramid and hit the buzzer. Winners get massages, yay!"

Jack and I share a look like, really? Near-death, and you get massages?

He shrugs. "I mean, it's better than a slap in the ass."

"True." I nod. "Okay, let's find one piece, just focus on one piece, then we can search for others that match it; otherwise, we'll be spread too thin."

Jack takes a deep breath.

"Three, two, one."

Jack and I run up the remaining stairs and into the first room and start searching around the fake grass and rocks for something—anything.

Jack stumbles behind a large fake boulder and makes a cross on his chest as a temple guard in full OG garb comes up behind him and lingers. The guard looks like he could be a Polynesian fire dancer except a bit more terrifying with what looks like a real spear.

They wouldn't give them real spears, right? I'm afraid to focus on it. It's over, Jack's going to be exposed to the guard, and we're going to lose. I just know it.

Jack takes a deep breath, reaches over, and grabs a rock next to him, then throws it in the opposite direction, grabs something from the ground, and mouths, "Run!"

He doesn't need to tell me twice. I chase after him while the temple guard is distracted and stumble onto my knees. The temple guard turns just as Jack grabs me and pulls me into his arms, slamming me back against the concrete wall as it turns into a secret room. Like an actual secret room that we just Indiana Jonesed.

"Whoa!" he shouts. "Look, there's another medallion over on that stone!"

I'm still trying to process the fact that I'm in his arms and that he actually risked his sanity to grab me. "You saved me."

"What?" He looks down, and I realize we're in the exact position as we were in college, with him pressing me against a wall and me wanting so much more than I will ever be able to admit. "You're my partner; no man left behind."

"But you're petrified."

He smiles down at me, a gorgeous smile that I'll remember until death; his hair glistens even as lit torches give the room a romantic ambiance lining the walls. "I was more afraid for you."

"That's…" I don't have words. "That's—"

He kisses me.

He kisses me in the exact spot where I know he's afraid, as if he's more afraid not to have me. I cling to him so hard I forget we're even playing a game until I hear a buzzer sound.

We pull away from each other.

"Kissing and sex later," he instructs with a wink. "Now we need that next medallion; we only have one more to find; we just have to hope it's for Zeus's temple."

"Right. Focus." I nod. "Right."

He kisses me again.

I cling to him.

I almost slap myself.

He just laughs and grabs my hand.

We run toward the medallion.

"Shit!" He doesn't pick it up. "It's the Babylonian Gardens."

"Well," I put my hands on my hips. "Let's pick it up just in case; maybe since this is a secret room, they have more in here? Kind of like a bonus thing?"

He frowns. "Wouldn't that be too easy?"

"Nope." I shake my head. "I refuse to even entertain the attempt to get into Max's brain. What if the secret room holds the rest?"

He nods. "Fine, so we grab a torch and just walk down that creepy hallway all confident like we're finding hidden treasures, and if we die…"

"We won't die," I remind him. "I mean, you might have a

slight accident, but we won't die; I think the spears are real, by the way, so you've been warned."

He stops and pulls the torch between us. "In what world was that helpful?"

I gulp. "Sorry, I was just preparing you!"

"Consider me fucking prepared!"

"Don't yell at me!"

"Don't scare me!'

"Ughhhhh!" I stomp my foot. "Grab the torch, and let's win this bitch!"

His eyes linger on my mouth before he pulls the torch away. What was that? Was he actually thinking about kissing me? Jack starts walking away from me, his torch lighting up the small hallway with its hieroglyphics on the walls. I notice that along that same wall is a trough. I stop in my tracks. "Jack, do you think that lights up?"

"Maybe?" He looks over at it. "I mean, it could be oil?"

"Only one way to find out," I say.

"Right, and get rid of our only torch blanketing us in darkness?"

I elbow him, "Why would they have running water through here?"

"Good point." He grumbles. "But when will this hallway end, and how good is the other team even doing? Do they get a hallway? Does this lead to intern hell? Will there be a moat? These are the things I can't get out of my head."

I sigh and drop the torch into what I think is oil, not brave enough to taste it, and just like I suspected, it lights up the entire hallway.

"Whoaaa…" Jack does a small turn. "Short hallway turns into tall hallway, look." He points up.

The hallway goes up at least fifteen feet, maybe more. And at the very end is a treasure and what looks like a swimming pool.

"Ready?" I hold out my hand. Jack grabs it.

It feels good.

It feels final.

He squeezes my hand back. "Another adventure? Hey, we're already in Hell; let's finish up before the sex."

"Always about the sex."

"Literally always." He pulls me into his arms and kisses me hard against the mouth, only to pull away. "How could I possibly do this without you and not want you every second, even with being as scared as I am?"

"Because you're focused on your dick?" I ask.

He shakes his head. "Because I'm focused on the girl."

My heart melts a little. "Don't say things like that; I might get the wrong idea."

He kisses my forehead. "Good."

And I really do melt as we walk hand in hand down to the end of the hallway. The pool is crystal blue and beautiful, something that belongs at a resort in Belize. And on the bottom of the pool are the rest of the medallions.

"I can't swim," he suddenly blurts.

I smack him. "Are you serious?"

His laugh makes me want to shove him into the pool. "No, but you should have seen your face."

"Hilarious." I cross my arms. "Okay, so how about you jump in, grab as many as you can, then I'll go?"

He takes a deep breath. "I mean, as long as we don't have predators—oh shit."

"What?"

He points. "Sharks, there are actual sharks in the water."

I'm petrified of sharks.

I think they all have killing on their minds.

I try to swallow. Why is my throat closing?

"Um," I tuck my hair behind my ears. "Yeah, um, let's rethink this."

"No time." Jack starts stripping out of his Silver Snake shirt. "I have to go in."

"YOU COULD DIE!" I yell.

He pauses mid-strip and looks over at me, and so do his glorious abs. "I'm not going to die; sharks don't just attack people."

"Do you not have Nat-Geo?"

He finishes removing his shirt and pats me on the head. "You'll be fine. I'll be fine. Just stay here. You helped with Olmec. I'll help here."

"Are you sure?" My voice is shaky. I feel weak, and then I turn around and see the opposing team rushing toward us. "Shit, shit, jump!"

Jack has no time to waste as he propels into the water and starts swimming around the sharks grabbing random medallions.

"You go," Jude yells. "I'll go next!"

Stacey jumps back. "Those are sharks!"

"This is student loan forgiveness!" he yells even louder. "Get the fuck in!"

He shoves her into the water, and she crashes near the medallions as Jack swims around and keeps grabbing.

I try not to panic when she thrashes next to him, but it's like the dude was on swim team as he gathers as many as he can and pulls them over his neck, then jumps back onto the side out of breath.

"Good job!" I yell.

I grab the necklace medallions and find the matches for both of the ones we have plus a third, then stare him down. "We have to sprint."

"Stacey, hurry the fuck up!" Jude yells.

"I was in track once," Jack teases.

I want to kiss him as we run back down the lit hallway and out of the secret room, and back into the main temple.

Now the hard part.

Putting them together in front of Olmec.

"You're up." Jack stumbles.

I quickly grab them from his neck and start forming them on the different pillars while Olmec starts shooting fire.

Jack freezes.

Jude and Stacey are suddenly out of the hallway.

"Hurry!" Jack yells.

"Trying!" I have one last medallion but can't figure out how they work together, and it's legit right in front of Olmec's face.

"Give it to me!" Jack grabs it out of my hands, places it in the correct area, and twists it.

Light bursts from around the temple.

"WINNERS! Jack and Ivy!"

We both hug while Jude and Stacey start yelling at each other, and I realize that while this may have been a bit insane—it was fun, it was worth it, and it was earned.

CHAPTER
Sixteen

Jack

"**J**ude was pisssssssed." I laugh again after we grab the trophy and make our way back into my apartment. Apparently, they're ours now after winning, on top of the bonus and in a weird change of fate.

We also both get a promotion.

Which also resulted in Jude yelling at Stacey and Max, telling them he'd send them to Olmec if they didn't cooperate with security.

All in all, a great yet weird day.

A great night.

A night that's about to maybe get better? Did she mean all those things? I feel dumb asking her, but she is next to me, and now I'm being awkward again after knowing Max gave us a full week off.

In his words, because of the trauma, we deserved it.

We found out later that several board members were betting on us like we were horses, but hey, at least we didn't die.

I pour Ivy a glass of wine; we're still in our Silver Snake shirts. She takes a sip and then shakes her head. "This is the most intense thing I've ever experienced, and I was proposed to my senior year of college then found him and my roommate in the same room after a late study night just, casually doing sixty-nine."

I almost spit out my wine. "I'm sorry, did I hear that right?"

"Unfortunately, yes."

"Does it make you feel better that my girlfriend for two years in college was sleeping with both her roommate, who happened to be a girl and me?"

"What?" she shrieks.

"She was too afraid to break it off, didn't ever find them together but was always weirdly suspicious of their long study dates." I shrug. "It was meant to be; I'm sure they'll be super happy. I'm still stuck on the whole you were proposed to in college; I mean, that's kind of young."

We move to the couch and sit with our wine putting our feet on the table. She shrugs. "I was ready for something bigger, and I think so often we get preached at like, go to school, get a job, get married, have kids."

"And look where that got us," I tease. "Legends of the hidden temple fighting for internships cheers to all the adults in our lives."

She laughs and lifts her rose. "Cheers."

We both sit in silence on the couch, the environment heavy with tension like we both know what we want to do, but for serious, what do we do? Do I just shake her hand and tell her goodnight, or do I go in for a kiss?

She takes a few sips, then puts the wine down on the table and stands. I'm curious about what she's doing, and then I'm tongue tied as she peels her shirt over her head, exposing her black sports bra, and starts taking off her leggings.

"Um, what are you doing?" I ask.

"Let's skip to the good part." She winks. "No more talk about exes, no more anything that makes us think about regrets or college and how horrible Olmec was."

"Is," I correct. "Is because you know Max is gonna keep that thing just to terrify me if I don't turn in reports on time."

She bursts out laughing, hands on curvy hips, facing me like a tasty snack I want to devour on repeat. "I'd like to see that."

"I would too if you promise sex afterward." I lean back.

Ivy gets up on my lap, straddling me. "That can be arranged."

"We're keeping Olmec. He'll be like our pet we pull out every time I want to thrust in, deal?"

"That's weird and yet cute."

"I'm a complicated partner, good old Silver Snakes." I hold up my hand for a high five; she grabs it and rolls her eyes.

We touch foreheads, and I kiss the shit out of her. I can't help it. I love her. I love everything about her. She's my perfect partner in crime, and I don't want to let her go.

Our kisses heat up until I have her on her back against the couch; it's big enough that we won't fall off unless I get too aggressive, and right now, I'm ready to start throwing pillows around, ripping my teeth into them in victory. I pin her hands up above her head, my hips already rocking against her as she starts to peel down the spandex I was forced to wear. When they get to my ankles, I kick them off, then work on getting my stupid shirt off my body.

Once I have it on the floor and am wearing nothing but my black boxer briefs, she slaps her hands across my abs and makes this growling sound. "How is this fair?"

"Slapping?"

"Abs, the V, the everything."

"Guess the other half of team Silver Snake's just lucky?"

She slaps me again; not gonna lie, I kind of like it. "Whyyyyyy though, why is that your thing? Can't blow jobs be your thing."

Her eyes narrow. "Are you saying they aren't?"

Oh shit. "No, no, that's not what I meant; I just meant hey, instead of slapping utilize that aggression into something that will turn us both on rather than make me want to tense up."

"Do blow jobs not tense you up?"

"Is this a trick question?"

She leans up and kisses me. "Dunno; what do you think?"

"I think," I kiss her again, deepening it. The feel of her hot mouth on mine is so addicting I have trouble finding words. "I think," I repeat, "I would be okay just kissing you for the rest of my life."

She jerks my head down, and our teeth nearly hit as her tongue shoves into my mouth, and then I'm gone, so gone; I just want to be here with her in this moment, throw all the past away.

I want to be with my partner.

"Get inside me," she demands breathlessly.

"That's a really sexy thing to say when I'm sitting here trying to decide how to do this without making things awkward."

She rolls down my briefs and grips me. "It's only awkward if you leave me hanging."

Her grip is rough, almost too rough. Fuck, I love it. I roll my hips into her palm and then slap her hand away and slam into her. Roughly yes, without any preparation, also yes, but she's fucking wet it doesn't matter, and I'm so hard I'm petrified I'm going to last like one point two seconds.

She's pinned beneath me, and I love it. I love that she's wrapping her legs around me, that she's sucking me in, making me hers.

"Keep doing that," I rasp. "Please, oh God, please, that's— You're so tight, you feel so hot." Emotions whirl with the physical act of what's happening like I know that this is it, but I'm terrified to say something. I keep moving, she keeps pulling, and my thrusts get more intense.

"Jack, please, please!" she begs, and I know what it's for, but I want this to last longer.

Then again, it's not about me.

I angle a bit differently and move my hand between her thighs, working her manually as I thrust. She comes apart all over my fingers with me inside. And it sparks my own release. We're a mess together. I don't think I've ever felt so spent.

I think she's about to say something super sweet when she looks up at me, smiles, and says, "Get rid of that damn stapler." Then she slaps me in the stomach.

Yay, another slap.

Okay, now I kind of like it.

"Never," I growl against her neck. "Now, let's go shower, clean up, burn the shirts, and do this again."

"**S**o, you really found them in your dorm senior year just going at it sixty-nine style?" I ask once in bed. I'm laughing because what the hell is wrong with this guy? I mean, seriously.

Ivy moves closer to me, throwing a leg over my body. "Yeah, and he was the one that was all like, missionary all the time, making me feel dumb for wanting more. Meanwhile, he's eating... yeah well, let's just not go there; we're no longer friends, and I think they got married."

"Good," I snap. "Because that means you're here. And mine."

I stare down at her gorgeously naked body and wonder what sort of blunt head trauma that idiot went through to not want to explore every corner of her body. Then I realize some guys, yes at times, ahem, me included, are just idiots, giant dicks, and have no clue how to treat a woman.

Smirking, I lean down and bite at her collarbone lightly and whisper against her skin. "Get on your knees."

"I'm not giving you another blow job." She huffs and crosses her arms as if she's offended when I know she loved every minute of it just like I did. I grab her by the hips, then flip her onto her stomach and say it again, this time with a light tap on her ass. "I wasn't talking about a blow job, but your offer is much appreciated; now, let me fuck you into this mattress like we're breaking up."

She peers over her shoulder, her hair causing a curtain across half her face. "When did we start dating?"

"When we won Legends of the Hidden Temple and Olmec didn't murder us, and you offered sex. It was the most romantic and terrifying moment of my life. One day we'll tell our grandchildren how we made it past the pit of doom and lived fuckily ever after while I did naughty things to grandma with a Nickelodeon medallion sliding between our bodies… 'there, oh right there, Jack, give it to me grandpa style—'"

She giggles. "Too far, you lost me at grandpa style."

"Weird, I thought it would be at the medallion part, dirty girl."

"Okay, Silver Snake…" She bursts out laughing while I slap her hard on the ass; it only makes her laugh harder. "I'm going to start strategically putting that shirt around the apartment just to give you nightmares."

"Oh, weird, when did we move in together?"

She slowly arches her body back toward me, giving me an excellent view of a curvy ass and legs for days. "When you asked me to get on my knees."

"Don't recall asking; it was more telling."

Her back arches.

And my Silver Snake does indeed appreciate it. I grip her thighs hard and pull her back into my lap. "Bet he never did this."

"Let me sit on him?" She shivers as I run my hands up and down her arms.

I grab a handful of hair and pull her face back, kissing down her neck before shoving her back onto the mattress and thrusting inside her with one smooth movement. "Any questions?"

"Zero." Her hands grip the pillows. "No questions, none, just lots of; how do you feel so good?"

"Silver Snake baby, Silver Snake."

"Go team." She laughs as I sink into her from behind. I grip her shoulders and tug her back onto me. I'm so deep I see stars. She wiggles her ass like she wants me to go deeper, but I'm like seconds away from losing it.

CHAPTER
Seventeen

Ivy

I wake up to Jack wrapped all around me; I love it. I love that we have the next week off and can just spend time getting to know each other after the chaos of the internships.

He's still snoring when the doorbell rings.

Frowning, I quickly get up and go to the door, snatching up a discarded sweatshirt and his briefs because, meh, why not? I have no choice!

I run over and slowly open the door.

Then nearly pass out.

It's him.

It's Connor.

My ex-fiancé.

He's holding a folding massage table.

The hell?

I open the door wider. "Are you at the right address?"

His eyes rake me over before he clears his throat and hands me a card that has Jack's and my address for the apartments written on it. "I um…" He frowns. "I'm sorry this is weird; I'm here to help the winners of the Internship for Emory Hotels?"

Shit.

"Yeah, um," I scratch my head and wonder what my hair even looks like. "That's us, I mean me and my partner Jack, but he's still sleeping; I guess you can come in… I'm not sure if he's going to want a massage, though. It was a rough few days for us."

Connor has his blond hair slicked back. His dimples are on full view, and his black T-shirt is tight around his broad shoulders. I don't look for a ring; I don't need that in my life. "Yeah, well, I work for Emory Hotels in Hospitality Services, so it's kind of my job to make sure you feel… good."

I almost cringe.

This feels bad.

And wrong.

I don't like it.

"Okay." I turn around a bit in a panic, trying to figure out what to do. "I guess put the table over there. I'm assuming you're the masseuse?"

"Career change." He smiles warmly, and all I can think about is sixty-nine, perfect. "I wanted something other than corporate. Turns out they like to make you want to jump off high buildings."

I snort laugh. "Yeah."

"So…" He eyes me up and down. "Should I just set up somewhere?"

"Yeah, sure, I mean, move the ottoman in the living room, and I'll grab Jack real quick."

Connor flinches a bit.

I'm sure he's assuming a lot.

Good. Let him.

Because I've moved on.

I sprint past him into the master. Jack's completely passed out, arms over his head, six-pack on full display, barely anything covering his dick, and damn, is he gorgeous.

I stick my tongue out at him while he's sleeping because how dare he, then I go over and shake him awake. "Hey, we got a surprise massage."

"No more blow jooobsssssss," he draws out. "I have nothing left in my body."

I cover my mouth to keep from laughing too loud. "It's not the kind with a happy ending, Jack."

"You gave me so many happy endings and beginnings."

My heart clenches.

I immediately want Connor to leave.

Deciding that's exactly what I'll do, I walk out into the living room and see he's quickly set up the gray table with nice white sheets and has his oils ready.

A massage sounds good.

But coming from him?

I finally check his left hand.

Ring.

Okay, well, that's progress.

"How's Sandra?." I ask.

His grin is wide. "Pregnant."

I actually smile at that. "Good. Congrats."

We're both quiet, all the things between us building up into this hurricane of emotion that neither of us want to even attempt to get into.

"So…" I fold my hands in front of me. "Jack's still sleeping, wouldn't wake up, not even for a blow job."

Yup, just said that out loud.

Connor starts choking; his cheeks turn red as he looks away and nods at the massage bed. "Then you can go first."

"Oh, no, no, no, no, that would be weird, and I'm actually not feeling sore." It's a lie. I really want to crawl into an ice bath.

"Get on," Connor says. "Jack can go next."

I'm tempted, seriously tempted, but it's an ex. Is that even normal?

"I'll be using products that have been put into the baskets in Emory Hotels, so it's really important, as you know to do proper R&D since, according to my report, you and the rest of the interns were using the products in order to see if they were a good investment."

Damn it.

"Yes," I admit. "We used them."

I think about the kissing. The pheromones.

I smile.

"That good, huh?" he asks.

"It was my job." I straighten. "You can use the products, I'll rate them, I'm keeping the briefs on, and no weirdness."

His smile is crooked. "That's fair."

"Good." I cross my arms.

"Good," he answers. "I guess I'll just go into the bathroom while you change?"

I start to sweat as he turns around, clearly knowing his way around the apartments. He goes to the spare and quietly shuts the door while I get on the table face down and try not to hyperventilate. I mean, it's a winning prize. A stupid massage. So why does it feel weird? Or why does it feel bad?

The door quietly opens. "You ready, Ivy?"

"Yeah," I choke out. "I think so." No. This feels wrong.

I start to get up and wrap the sheet around me right when Jack walks out of the master, all sleepy-eyed, and stumbles into the living room. "What the fuck?"

"It's a prize!" I all but shout. "And I didn't know it was Connor. You were; first, he works for the company, didn't know, but I didn't want to wake you!"

Why am I shouting? Even Connor is wincing.

Jack frowns. "Should I know a Connor?" He's wearing a pair of low-slung gray Nike sweats that make him look like a god; it's nearly impossible to look away. "Also, you left bed way too early; gonna spank you later."

I gape.

Connor gapes.

"What?" Jack shrugs. "This little sex kitten wore me out last night, bro, I'm not even trying to brag, but you've never done a sixty-nine until you've done one with her."

I. Want. To. Die.

He knows. How does he know? Did I mention Connor's name? Did I? Maybe? But even then, there is more than one in this godforsaken world!!!!

"Oh, um…" Connor scratches his head, cheeks red. "G-good for you guys."

"I mean," Jack keeps walking toward me, and not gonna lie, you can totally see his dick through his gray sweatpants, and it would put any dick to shame, and now I can't stop staring, and Connor looks very interested in our curtains. "She's just… fire. I can't wait to marry you, baby."

My mouth drops open.

Jack winks.

I love him.

I truly love him.

I hate him.

But I love him.

"And all those little grandkids we'll have, you know, after our two point five kids and white picket fence, they'll know all about how we just hammered our way through our internship, each made six figures with a 401k and just lived our lives sending them to private school, vacationing at your favorite places, Turkey, Belize, Hawaii, I can't wait to go back."

He's so laying it on thick.

And while I want to grab his discarded stapler and push it into his head, I also see only him.

Just him.

"We don't need massages, bro." Jack looks over his shoulder. "If anyone gets to massage her, it's gonna be me. But thanks for coming; I'll help you get everything put away; I know it's heavy."

Oh, damn.

He just insulted Connor's ability to lift heavy objects.

I could kiss him.

"Do I know you from somewhere?" Connor asks Jack, his arms crossed.

"Yup." Jack makes his way over to me, presses a heated kiss to my mouth then pulls back. "I'm the guy that noticed."

"Huh?" Connor asks. "What do you mean?"

"The guy that noticed how perfect she was." Jack's eyes go to Connor's left hand. "Glad you noticed one too. Now, let's get this broken down so I can show my girl how much I notice, yeah?"

Connor actually laughs, then nods his head. "Did not expect this at eight this morning, yet here I am." He walks toward Jack and holds out his hand to shake. "Treat her the way she deserves. Be better than her last ex." He peers around Jack. "He was such a dick."

"A total dick." Jack laughs.

"God, this was such a setup, wasn't it?" Connor asks. "Was this Max again? Why is he so fucking bored?"

"RIGHT?" Jack yells. "I mean torture other people!"

"One day," Connor sounds haunted. "Actually, no, you don't deserve that trauma. I hope you guys are happy. And dude…" He looks down at Jack's dick and shakes his head. "Didn't know it was possible."

My turn to peer around Jack. "It is. It was. It will be."

Connor laughs again. "All right, so my non-work here is done. Good luck with Max. Try not to die."

"Almost did." Jack shudders. "Twice."

"Peace be with you, my friend." Connor slaps him on the shoulder, and it's not even weird; it's like he gets it, and I finally have that weird closure I've always needed.

"Be happy," I say once they fold the massage table back up and he's on his way out.

He nods and looks between us. "What a Monday."

"Should have seen us on Sunday." Jack winks.

"I have a feeling it would have been illegal in most states." He grabs his stuff, the door shuts, and I just jump onto Jack.

"Whoa, whoa, what's that for?"

"For wearing gray sweatpants and making his dick feel small, for making my heart feel big, and for loving me even though I want to kill you half the time."

"Aw…" Jack flicks me in the nose lightly. "That's the sweetest thing anyone has ever said to me. Does that mean the stapler gets to come back?"

I kiss him hard on the mouth and then bite down on his lower lip. "Never."

"Damn it, I had high hopes."

"High hope this," I say as I pry myself away, get onto my feet then drop to my knees. "I mean, I do still owe you."

"I mean, if you have to pay up, I won't complain."

I cup his balls.

He nearly kicks me. "I'm sensitive; you were hard on me last night."

"Hard." I laugh.

"So. Hard." He thrusts his cock in my direction, and I take him in my mouth, sucking deep, then pull away. "Whoa, what's wrong?"

I get up quickly and turn. "Gonna have to chase the girl, Jack."

"I've chased her a long time," he points out. "And I'll capture her. Every. Time."

I don't run far.

I make it a few feet.

And then I'm on my back, in missionary position, realizing that it can be pretty great with the right person, with my legs up on his shoulders and his eyes locked on mine.

Yeah, it can be pretty great.

This whole Office Date thing.

Just don't tell Max.

CHAPTER
Eighteen

Max

"**Y**ou're a genius, sir." Dustin creeps up my ass again.

Max swats him away and stares at the kiddos in the boardroom.

They're in love.

And I'm a friggin' matchmaker.

It's confirmed.

He smiles as Dustin holds the folders showing them their starting salary and the apartments they'll be keeping unless they want to move into one.

"I don't know how you do it," Dustin says as he wipes a tear. "I hate you half the time but look at them."

The interns are holding hands.

His work here is done.

Just another office romance.

All because of him.

"By the way," Dustin says as he hands Max a report. "The Board of Directors said they really liked the physicality of the temple; maybe next year we should do something like—"

"Shhh, shhh, shhh, little bird." Max puts a finger to Dustin's lips. "You know how the games go. The old interns pick them out. I merely orchestrate the love."

Dustin rolls his eyes.

"Saw that." Max adjusts his tie. "Now go feed the gecko, don't forget about the goat, and remember not to breathe too heavy around me. It's agitating."

"I have allergies."

"Excuses." Max grins. "Oh, and the goat has the shits."

Dustin curses as Max walks into the boardroom. "Winners, let me introduce you to some of your co-workers. First line of business now that you've fallen in love and decided to be giant winners—you get to pick next year's games."

Jack jumps out of his seat. "THIS IS THE BEST MOMENT OF MY LIFE."

Ivy kicks him. "Really?"

"Second?"

She kicks him again. "Fifth, tenth, damn it, Ivy, I want to torture people!"

Max laughs. "Knew I picked the right people. Now stop kissing long enough to sign your contracts, and kiddos... make it rain pain."

Max has never, in his career, and years later will admit to this, seen a former intern look more evil in the way he smiled.

Good.

Ah, little grasshopper.

Fantastic.

WANT MORE RVD?

Did you enjoy Office Date?
Then check out these other Romantic Comedies!

Office Hate (Mark & Olivia's story)

The Consequence Series
The Consequence of Loving Colton (Colton & Milo's story)
The Consequence of Revenge (Max & Becca's story)
The Consequence of Seduction (Reid & Jordan's story)
The Consequence of Rejection (Jason & Maddy's story)

The Bet Series
The Bet (Travis & Kacey's story)
The Wager (Jake & Char Lynn's story)
The Dare (Jace & Beth Lynn's story)

ACKNOWLEDGMENTS

Without God or Jill, this book would not have ever gotten written, lol. It was something I was working on while working on scripts, tv stuff, and other publishing deadlines and was constantly in the back of my head needing to get done. Finally, I was put on a schedule (again, thanks Jill!), and here we are!

I'm so pumped to bring you this silly, crazy little Legends of the Temple/Squid Games fun. We all need a little chaos in our lives when it comes to books, you know what I mean? Where books are just silly and fun and no stress. Hopefully, this was that book for you.

Thanks to Valentine PR, my agent Nicole, my team of amazing, incredible women, and Rachel's New Rockin Readers on Facebook. So thankful.

Love you all.

Thank you for reading!

ABOUT THE
Author

Rachel Van Dyken is the #1 *New York Times, Wall Street Journal,* and *USA Today* bestselling author of over 100 books ranging from contemporary romance to paranormal. With over four million copies sold, she's been featured in Forbes, US Weekly, and USA Today. Her books have been translated in more than 15 countries. She was one of the first romance authors to have a Kindle in Motion book through Amazon publishing and continues to strive to be on the cutting edge of the reader experience. She keeps her home in the Pacific Northwest with her husband, adorable sons, naked cat, and dog. For more information about her books and upcoming events, visit www.RachelVanDykenAuthor.com.

ALSO BY
Rachel Van Dyken

Eagle Elite

Elite (Nixon & Trace's story)
Elect (Nixon & Trace's story)
Entice (Chase & Mil's story)
Elicit (Tex & Mo's story)
Bang Bang (Axel & Amy's story)
Enforce (Elite + from the boys POV)
Ember (Phoenix & Bee's story)
Elude (Sergio & Andi's story)
Empire (Sergio & Val's story)
Enrage (Dante & El's story)
Eulogy (Chase & Luciana's story)
Exposed (Dom & Tanit's story)
Envy (Vic & Renee's story)

Elite Bratva Brotherhood

RIP (Nikolai & Maya's story)
Debase (Andrei & Alice's story)

Mafia Royals Romances
Royal Bully (Asher & Claire's story)
Ruthless Princess (Serena & Junior's story
Scandalous Prince (Breaker & Violet)
Destructive King (Asher & Annie)
Mafia King (Tank & Kartini)
Fallen Royal (Maksim's story)
Broken Crown (King's story)

Cruel Summer Trilogy
Summer Heat (Marlon & Ray's story)
Summer Seduction (Marlon & Ray's story)
Summer Nights (Marlon & Ray's story)

Wingmen Inc.
The Matchmaker's Playbook (Ian & Blake's story)
The Matchmaker's Replacement (Lex & Gabi's story)

Bro Code
Co-Ed (Knox & Shawn's story)
Seducing Mrs. Robinson (Leo & Kora's story)
Avoiding Temptation (Slater & Tatum's story)
The Setup (Finn & Jillian's story)

Liars, Inc
Dirty Exes (Colin, Jessie & Blaire's story)
Dangerous Exes (Jessie & Isla's story)

Curious Liaisons
Cheater (Lucas & Avery's story)
Cheater's Regret (Thatch & Austin's story)

Covet
Stealing Her (Bridge & Isobel's story)
Finding Him (Julian & Keaton's story)

Players Game
Fraternize (Miller, Grant and Emerson's story)
Infraction (Miller & Kinsey's story)
M.V.P. (Jax & Harley's story)

The Dark Ones Series
The Dark Ones (Ethan & Genesis's story)
Untouchable Darkness (Cassius & Stephanie's story)
Dark Surrender (Alex & Hope's story)
Darkest Temptation (Mason & Serenity's story)
Darkest Sinner (Timber & Kyra's story)

Ruin Series
Ruin (Wes Michels & Kiersten's story)
Toxic (Gabe Hyde & Saylor's story)
Fearless (Wes Michels & Kiersten's story)
Shame (Tristan & Lisa's story)

Seaside Series
Tear (Alec, Demetri & Natalee's story)
Pull (Demetri & Alyssa's story)
Shatter (Alec & Natalee's story)
Forever (Alec & Natalee's story)
Fall (Jamie Jaymeson & Pricilla's story)
Strung (Tear + from the boys POV)
Eternal (Demetri & Alyssa's story)

Seaside Pictures
Capture (Lincoln & Dani's story)
Keep (Zane & Fallon's story)
Steal (Will & Angelica's story)
All Stars Fall (Trevor & Penelope's story)
Abandon (Ty & Abigail's story)
Provoke (Braden & Piper's story)
Surrender (Andrew & Bronte's story)

Red Card
Risky Play (Slade & Mackenzie's story)
Kickin' It (Matt & Parker's story)

The Consequence Series
The Consequence of Loving Colton (Colton & Milo's story)
The Consequence of Revenge (Max & Becca's story)
The Consequence of Seduction (Reid & Jordan's story)
The Consequence of Rejection (Jason & Maddy's story)

The Bet Series
The Bet (Travis & Kacey's story)
The Wager (Jake & Char Lynn's story)
The Dare (Jace & Beth Lynn's story)

The Bachelors of Arizona
The Bachelor Auction (Brock & Jane's story)
The Playboy Bachelor (Bentley & Margot's story)
The Bachelor Contract (Brant & Nikki's story)

Standalone Titles
My Summer in Seoul (Grace's story)
Office Hate (Mark & Olivia's story)
A Crown for Christmas (Fitz & Phillipa's story)
Every Girl Does It (Preston & Amanda's story)
Compromising Kessen (Christian & Kessen's story)
Divine Uprising (Athena & Adonis's story)
The Parting Gift — written with Leah Sanders (Blaine and Mara's story)

Rachel Van Dyken & M. Robinson
Mafia Casanova (Romeo Sinacore's story)
Falling for the Villain (Juliet Sinacore's story)

Kathy Ireland & Rachel Van Dyken
Fashion Jungle

London Fairy Tales
Upon a Midnight Dream (Stefan & Rosalind's story)
Whispered Music (Dominique & Isabelle's story)
The Wolf's Pursuit (Hunter & Gwendolyn's story)
When Ash Falls (Ashton & Sofia's story)

Renwick House
The Ugly Duckling Debutante (Nicholas & Sara's story)
The Seduction of Sebastian St. James (Sebastian & Emma's story)
The Redemption of Lord Rawlings (Phillip & Abigail's story)
An Unlikely Alliance (Royce & Evelyn's story)
The Devil Duke Takes a Bride (Benedict & Katherine's story)

Waltzing With The Wallflower — written with Leah Sanders
Waltzing with the Wallflower (Ambrose & Cordelia)
Beguiling Bridget (Anthony & Bridget's story)
Taming Wilde (Colin & Gemma's story)

www.rachelvandykenauthor.com